Mark frowned as her gaze slid to her throbbing finger.

Without asking her permission, he lifted her hand as cautiously as if it were made of milkweed floss. "Guess I'm too late. It's in deep, ain't so?"

"*Ja.*" Were her fingers trembling, or were his as he bent toward her?

"Don't move."

"What?"

He pinched the sore spot on her index finger, then raised his head, grinning. "Got it." He held up a teeny piece of wood.

Kirsten was amazed. The sliver had felt as big as a log. "*Danki.* I thought I was going to have to wait until I could get home and use a needle and tweezers."

"You can't work in a woodworking shop for long without becoming skilled at dealing with splinters." He laughed as he released her hand.

Something sharp pierced her. Not a splinter this time, but a sense of regret he wasn't holding her hand any longer.

Was she out of her mind? Four men had been eager to hold her hand, and she'd been thrilled to have them do so. Then each of them had dropped her hand and walked away…

Jo Ann Brown loves stories with happily-ever-after endings. A former military officer, she is thrilled to write about finding that forever love all over again with her characters. She and her husband (her real hero who knows how to fix computer problems quickly when she's on deadline) divide their time between Western Massachusetts and Amish country in Pennsylvania. She loves hearing from readers, so drop her a note at joannbrownbooks.com.

Books by Jo Ann Brown

Love Inspired

Amish of Prince Edward Island

Building Her Amish Dream
Snowbound Amish Christmas

Green Mountain Blessings

An Amish Christmas Promise
An Amish Easter Wish
An Amish Mother's Secret Past
An Amish Holiday Family

Amish Spinster Club

The Amish Suitor
The Amish Christmas Cowboy
The Amish Bachelor's Baby
The Amish Widower's Twins

Visit the Author Profile page at LoveInspired.com for more titles.

Snowbound Amish Christmas

Jo Ann Brown

LOVE INSPIRED
INSPIRATIONAL ROMANCE

LOVE INSPIRED®
INSPIRATIONAL ROMANCE

ISBN-13: 978-1-335-58530-1

Snowbound Amish Christmas

Love Inspired
22 Adelaide St. West, 41st Floor
Toronto, Ontario M5H 4E3, Canada
www.LoveInspired.com

Printed in U.S.A.

What shall we then say to these things?
If God be for us, who can be against us?
—*Romans* 8:31

For Matt Weaver and Cindy Barton

Thanks for helping us find our new old home
in Amish country!

Chapter One

Shushan Bay
Prince Edward Island, Canada

Where was she?

Mark Yutzy paused in his pacing by the window in the front room of the creaky old farmhouse, his home for the past eight months. He scanned the road separating his farm from the bay. The ticking clock was a constant reminder the meeting he was supposed to have with the owner of the cleaning service he'd hired should have happened a half hour ago. He could hear his youngest brother, Daryn Yutzy, eating in the kitchen.

Frowning, Mark folded his arms and glared out the window. He'd asked Daryn to wait until Mark could share the meal. *Share* being the important word, because his sixteen-year-old brother could polish off a whole meal meant for two and ask for dessert. Daryn was a self-absorbed teenager who did the bare minimum Mark asked him to do around the farm. After a summer of trying to adjust the boy's attitude, Mark hadn't gotten anywhere.

Mark heard a spoon scrape against ceramic and

hoped there would be something left for him. Daryn was helping himself to another serving of the beef and noodles sent over by their mutual cousin Mattie Albrecht. No, she was Mattie Kuhns, married three months. She often made extra casseroles and brought them to him and their other cousins, the Kuepfer brothers.

The four of them, Mattie, Lucas Kuepfer, Juan Kuepfer and himself, had come to Prince Edward Island in the spring to make new lives. Like a family of pioneers, they'd left Ontario for a new Amish settlement in Canada's smallest province. They'd become partners in a farm shop and three farms. Last spring, Mattie, who at thirty-one was more than a year older than he was, had done the impossible and gotten the store off the ground, in spite of a lot of challenges. Its profits had provided for them during the summer while they waited for the fields to yield their harvests.

They were going to succeed. Mark wouldn't accept anything less than complete success. Not failing had been his motto for as long as he could remember. It was a lesson *Mamm* and *Daed* hoped their wayward, youngest son would learn from Mark, and he wasn't going to let them down. So much had depended on this harvest, but Mark was accustomed to the pressure of building a prosperous business. In fact, if anyone had asked him, he would have said he thrived on stress.

Nobody had asked because, other than church Sundays, he seldom saw anyone other than his brother and his cousins, who were working as hard as he was. The potato harvest was in, and he'd arranged with a broker to buy the majority of the crop. The rest would be going to the family's farm shop. The money from selling potatoes would allow them to begin over again when spring returned to the island.

A motion caught his eye. Someone was coming along the road by the bay. The water sparkled in moonlight, though a glow from the setting sun lingered in the west. He frowned as a flashlight matched steady steps. Didn't the Petersheim family live to the east, closer to the end of the island? The woman was coming from the opposite direction. Had she let other clients make her late?

That wasn't any way to run a business. Not in his opinion.

An assertive knock on the front door jarred Mark's thoughts. He went to the door. When he threw it open, the salt-scented air and the November chill rushed in along with the aroma of something sweet. Jasmine? Lilacs? Roses? He couldn't say. He'd never paid attention to flowers, focusing instead on field crops.

"Mark Yutzy?" the woman asked in a pleasing, low-pitched voice.

He stared. He couldn't help himself. When he'd arranged to hire a cleaning company so he could focus on his harvest, he'd met with an older woman. Hadn't she said her name was Helga? She hadn't been as tall as this woman whose dark brown eyes were level with his gaze, and he wasn't a short man. Her hair, pulled back beneath her conical *kapp*, was so black it disappeared in the thick twilight. She was a generation younger than the other woman, much closer to his twenty-nine years.

Where had he seen her before? The answer came from memory. Before the Celtic Knoll Farm Shop had opened, the community had joined together for a work frolic there. This pretty woman had been among the volunteers who made it possible for the shop to open on time.

"Are you Mark Yutzy?" she asked into the strained silence. "If you aren't, could you let Mark know I'm here?"

Her simple question jerked him out of his thoughts. "*Ja*, I'm Mark Yutzy. And you're—"

"Kirsten Petersheim, owner of Ocean Breezes Cleaning."

"You? I thought a woman named Helga owned it."

"Helga is my *aenti* and one of my employees. I own the company. I assumed you knew." Her tone suggested he was a potato or two short of a bushel. "You sent me a note."

"I did, but…" He'd given it to Daryn to deliver, and he wondered how his brother had known Kirsten Petersheim was the owner of the company. He cringed. When he asked Daryn a question, his brother saw it as an unprovoked attack in an ongoing war and lashed back. To be honest, Mark was exhausted with walking on eggshells around the kid, hoping there wouldn't be another eruption that ended with Daryn stomping off and the work being left to Mark. *Lord, help me find more patience.* He'd prayed that a dozen times a day every day since Daryn's arrival.

When he realized Kirsten was waiting for him to finish, he said, "*Ja*, I sent you a note."

"A note deman—asking me to come and speak with you this evening." Her lips tightened, and color splashed on her cheeks. She was embarrassed she'd almost said "demanding."

He felt a pinch of self-consciousness when he thought about the note. *It is imperative we meet at my house today at 6 pm to discuss the continuation of your services.*

No wonder she nearly said "demanding." He'd been in a hurry…and annoyed, never a *gut* time to write a note.

Watch what you say to others because wrong words linger longer than you might expect. He'd learned to heed that warning from his *daed*, but somehow, in his urgency to get the harvest in and get it sold, he'd forgotten.

His *daed* had offered plenty of *gut* counsel throughout Mark's youth, but nothing about being successful. Clifford Yutzy hadn't had much skill as a farmer and fewer as a woodworker. Well-liked by plain and *Englisch* neighbors, the furniture shop had survived for many years because customers enjoyed coming to his shop and chatting with him.

Everything had changed when Mark, barely fourteen years old, built his first variable desk and chair set. The unit could be arranged in a multitude of ways to suit anyone from a short *kind* to a tall adult. It also allowed for multiple uses, including a top that could be raised or lowered. After he'd put it on display in *Daed*'s shop, it'd been seen by a vacationing Toronto designer. When she asked permission to take photos, Mark couldn't have imagined the desk would become the centerpiece of an article in the lifestyle section of Toronto's largest newspaper and would have been picked up by wire services throughout Canada and the United States. *Daed*'s store had filled with customers, and the phone had rung constantly with orders for Mark's design.

That success had changed him and his family. He continued to design innovative furniture, each piece becoming more popular than the previous one. They'd hired more woodworkers until over two hundred people were employed at Yutzy Family Furniture. Money was no longer a worry. His four sisters and his three brothers had each been given the down payment on a home when they married.

Mark had saved his share of the profits. For years, he'd imagined buying a farm far from the bustle of the shop. When he'd heard about the new settlements in Prince Edward Island, he'd jumped at the opportunity, sinking every penny he had in land and equipment along with his cousins. He longed to make this endeavor a success too. He must focus on that and helping his youngest brother stop thinking the world revolved around him.

Otherwise, he asked himself, why would he have bothered to get someone to come in and clean the house? He'd had no idea how many hours each day, seven days a week, farmwork would consume.

"*Komm* in," he said, realizing he'd left Kirsten standing on the porch as the evening grew colder. The second week of November in Prince Edward Island felt more like winter than fall.

"*Danki.*" She stepped into the tight entry. The broad staircase, as straight and solid as a spruce tree, took up most of the space.

"You're late. I thought six o'clock would be a convenient time for you."

When she flinched, he realized he'd let frustration sharpen his voice. What had happened to the customer service skills he'd honed in *Daed*'s shop? Wait a minute! *He* was the customer. She was supposed to be making sure she fulfilled his expectations.

Her eyes flashed, but her tone remained cool. "Six would have been fine most nights, but I was delayed by my boss."

"Your boss? I thought Ocean Breezes Cleaning was your company."

"It is, but I've also been working at the Sea Gull Holiday Cottages along the bay road toward Shushan."

"I see." He was impressed. She must have a clear head for business, something he had to admire. Not quitting her previous job while she got her new company up and running made a lot of sense. If his *daed* had had as much sense years ago, the family would have avoided years of wondering where their next meal would come from. Not that the plain community would have allowed them to starve…if they'd had any idea of how precarious the situation was. His parents had too much pride to ask for help.

Foolish *hochmut*, he'd heard his older siblings say.

He agreed. Pride was stupid as well as a sin. As far as he could see, those who had the least reason for *hochmut* clung to it most closely. He didn't want to be one of those people, which was why he didn't intend to fail.

Kirsten adjusted the black purse hanging from her shoulder. "Your note suggested you aren't happy with our work."

"Let me show you."

She nodded when he gestured toward the bathroom past the stairs. When he led the way, he heard the soft sound of her black sneakers on the bare floors. The wood needed refinishing, but it, like so many other things, would have to wait until he was paid for the potatoes he'd harvested with Daryn's sporadic help.

Mark opened the bathroom door and stepped to one side to let Kirsten peer in. Again that enticing scent teased his nose. Lilacs, he decided, recalling the sweet smell from spring.

"Oh, my!" she gasped when she looked inside.

"Do you consider this cleaned?" He could have phrased it better, but the aromas from the kitchen warned him if he didn't get done soon, Daryn would have finished off the whole casserole before Mark could get a single bite.

Seeing Kirsten's mouth draw into a straight line, he almost apologized. He stopped himself, reminding himself he'd paid to have his house cleaned, and it hadn't been. So why was he feeling guilty about complaining?

Kirsten didn't look in Mark Yutzy's direction. She'd hoped the imperious tone of his note was an aberration, but he was as abrupt in person.

What a peculiar way for a plain man to act!

You've encountered other plain men who didn't act as expected. She didn't need her memories to remind her. Somehow, she'd attracted the wrong men. The day she'd left Ontario was the day she'd vowed she was going to keep men at arm's length, so she wasn't hurt and embarrassed again.

She couldn't think about the past. She had to focus on dealing with Mark Yutzy. It might have been simpler if he wasn't so *gut*-looking. No man should have such sturdy shoulders and such amazing bright blue eyes that were even with hers, something she wasn't accustomed to because she was usually the tallest person in any room. His hair was the palest blond she'd ever seen, and it was the perfect foil for his tanned skin. His self-confidence and intensity were something she could respect, and crinkles by his eyes suggested he was a man who smiled often.

Just not with her.

Enough!

He wasn't happy with the job her cousin had done. Neither was she. As she looked around the tight space, she wondered if Janelle had even come into the bathroom. Her cousin was fifteen, so she was capable of cleaning the house, so why wasn't it sparkling as Kirsten had expected?

Again Kirsten wondered if it'd been a mistake to hire her cousin and her *aenti* Helga to work for her. Kirsten had hoped that having her family's help would help her balance her company along with her work at Sea Gull Holiday Cottages. The hours there were long and the work hard and the pay not great, but Kirsten had stayed while starting her business. What else could she have done when the family needed money? Kirsten had left Ontario last year at *Aenti* Helga's invitation in the wake of being stood up at her and Eldon's wedding. Nobody could have guessed *Onkel* Stanley would die from a heart attack, at fifty, the week after their arrival on Prince Edward Island. Kirsten and *Aenti* Helga had to find work to provide for her *aenti*'s two *kinder*, Janelle and Theodore.

Theo was twelve and in school. He did his best to help with chores on their small farm, milking the trio of cows morning and night as well as tending to the pig. He couldn't work the fields alone.

"Next year," Theo often said, and she wanted to put her arms around him each time. He shouldn't have been worried about anything beyond his studies and whether he'd hit a home run during the next baseball game. He hadn't had time to mourn his *daed*. None of them had.

Keeping her sigh silent, Kirsten had to step sideways to get through the narrow space between the sink and a claw-foot tub. Had Janelle found it impossible to angle herself to clean the fixtures?

Maybe, but that didn't explain why the inside of the sink hadn't been wiped. Neither had the ugly green tiles.

"Be careful," Mark said when she edged past the tub. "One of the feet is cracked, and it rocks."

"Are you keeping it?"

"No. It doesn't fit us. We can't turn around in it." Before she could wonder who "we" were, he went on, "Daryn—he's my brother—grouses he has to stand with one foot in front of the other when taking a shower."

"It is narrow." She forced her gaze to remain on the stained tub and not shift toward the handsome man standing in the doorway.

Kirsten pulled out a small book and opened it to the page where she'd written Mark's name. She began to list the shortcomings she could see in the cleaning. She asked Mark to add his concerns, and she wrote each one, even when he complained how the toilet paper had been left on the toilet instead of being put on the holder.

"Any other problems?" she asked when he paused.

"*Ja.*"

"In the bathroom?"

When he didn't answer, she looked up to see him shake his head. She tried to look away, but wasn't fast enough. Her gaze collided with his bright blue eyes and stuck like chewing gum under a table.

She wasn't sure how long she would have stood, frozen by the shock of sensations she'd vowed never to feel again, if someone hadn't called, "Mark, are you going to eat? If you're not, can I finish off the casserole?"

"My youngest brother," Mark said with the first hint she'd seen of a grin.

"A teenager?"

"*Ja.* How did you know?"

"My cousin Theo will be thirteen next year, and he can eat more than the rest of us together."

Mark nodded. "Sounds familiar."

Forcing her eyes away from his enticing smile, she looked at her notebook. She'd come to Prince Edward Island to escape her horrible history with men. She tightened her grip on the notebook, but loosened it when she realized she was bending the metal spiral. She'd been a fool for four men already, believing they cared about her. Each time, she'd been wrong, but never so wrong as when she'd been jilted in front of everyone she loved. She'd made a vow to God and to herself that she wouldn't put herself in that situation ever again. The idea of living the rest of her life as an *alt maedel* was preferable to being the focus of shocked and horrified looks when three hundred wedding guests realized the groom was nowhere to be found.

She'd hoped coming to Prince Edward Island would be enough to chase the memories from her head. She wondered if anywhere on Earth was far enough to escape them. Maybe not, but she wasn't going to compound her humiliation by admiring another *gut*-looking man.

Realizing Mark was waiting for her to go on, Kirsten said, "We've covered the problems in the bathroom. What else?"

"The rest of the house as well, but it would take too long to point out every problem."

She fought to keep her expression serene. Janelle had said last night she'd spent four hours at the Yutzy house. What had she been doing? It wasn't like the *Englisch* house where her cousin wanted to work around three in the afternoon, so she could watch television. The Yutzys were plain and didn't have a TV.

"I'm sorry your house wasn't cleaned properly," Kirsten replied. "I'll be discussing this with my employee. She's been trying her best, but she's new. Because of the problems, your next cleaning will be free."

"Free?" He stared at her in amazement.

"Do you have a problem with free?" She arched her brows. "It's not like I plan to pay *you* to let us clean your home."

She wanted to take back the words as soon as she spoke them. They weren't appropriate with clients. If she hadn't been so annoyed with Janelle's slapdash work… No, she couldn't blame her cousin. Standing so close to this handsome man whose bright blue eyes had a way of shifting color along with the light was dangerous to her hard-fought-for equilibrium.

She had to end this conversation.

Now.

Mark stared. Was Kirsten joking? He wanted to believe she was, yet nothing in her voice or on her calm face suggested she was anything but serious.

When he didn't answer, unsure how to respond, she continued, "So Janelle will come a week from Wednesday at the regular time. I assume that won't be a problem."

He shook his head.

"*Gut.*" She closed her notebook and walked out of the bathroom. She paused by the front door. Pulling a business card from her apron pocket, she handed it to him. "You can reach me at this number. *Guten owed.*"

He didn't have a chance to return her "good evening" before she'd opened the door and was gone. He couldn't remember the last time he'd gotten so few words in during a business meeting.

Mark walked into the pea-green kitchen, which, like the bathroom, had been cleaned with little more than a lick and a promise. The floorboards were uneven, and damp stained one corner near the door. A block of wood beneath one leg of the table kept it from wobbling.

He felt numb as he paused in the doorway. He hadn't discussed anything but the bathroom with Kirsten, so why did he feel as if he'd gone two rounds with a heavyweight champion?

He'd been handling the discussion okay until Daryn had intruded to ask—*actually ask*—if he could finish the casserole. He didn't fool himself by thinking Daryn was beginning to change. He'd made that mistake twice before. His youngest brother was up to something or wanted something.

"That went well." Daryn grinned. His brother, at sixteen, had arms and legs that seemed to grow an inch every day. He looked no bigger around than the nearly empty casserole dish on the table. His blond hair needed to be cut, and pale fuzz edged his cheeks, showing he hadn't shaved in a while.

"You think so?" Mark growled.

Maybe if he'd been a rebellious teen, he'd understand his brother better. When he was Daryn's age, he'd been working a dozen hours a day every day but Sunday. Some days longer. He'd gotten a lot of satisfaction from a job well done. He wished he could instill that in Daryn, but nothing he'd said had stuck.

"Sarcasm doesn't suit you, bro." Daryn laughed. "Don't you know the old saying about honey and vinegar?" He shoveled another forkful of noodles into his mouth and eyed the rest of the casserole.

"Which is *gut* if I wanted to catch flies. I want to have this house cleaned as I've paid for it to be."

"She said Janelle would clean for free. You can't beat free, ain't so?"

He frowned, pausing as he was reaching for the dish and realized there was less in it than he'd thought. *Gut* thing he had peanut butter in the cupboard. His stomach turned. He'd been eating too many peanut butter sandwiches lately. "Were you eavesdropping?"

Daryn's smile vanished, and his shoulders rose. He flung a hand toward the wide arch between the two rooms. "It's not easy *not* to hear everything. The walls here are paper thin."

"I know." He hated his consoling tone, but he was too tired to deal with his brother. No wonder *Daed* and

Mamm had wanted to get Daryn away from his friends and the bad habits he was picking up in Ontario. Trying to lighten his voice, he added, "I hear you snoring every night."

He held his breath, then released it when Daryn's grin returned. "Funny. I thought it was *you* who sounded like an asthmatic chain saw."

Spooning the little bit of noodles left in the casserole dish onto his plate, Mark sighed. He was relieved when his brother resumed eating as if he hadn't seen food in a month.

Mark looked at the meager pile of noodles on his plate. Rising, he went to the cupboard and pulled out the few pieces of bread left in the bag. He grabbed the jar of peanut butter and frowned. By its weight, he could tell the jar was empty. Putting it aside, he opened the refrigerator and found orange marmalade, one of the few things his brother didn't like, and brought it to the table.

"What's wrong?" asked Daryn, startling him again.

Knowing he'd be smart to keep the conversation going, so maybe he'd get some idea of why Daryn was being pleasant, Mark replied, "On edge."

"Because she's pretty?"

"What?" He shook his head. "It's not that."

Daryn chuckled. "It would be for me. Nothing puts me on edge more than a pretty girl."

Deciding it'd be best to ignore the comment, Mark took a deep swig of the root beer Daryn had poured for him. He lowered the glass. "Wow, this is *gut*! Where did you get it? At Mattie's store?"

"No, a friend dropped by with it. Great, ain't so?"

"Ja." He took another sip. "You should tell your friend to talk to Mattie about carrying his root beer at the store. He's got a winner."

"She."

"She what?"

"My friend is a she, so it's *her* root beer."

"Daryn, I know you're young, and girls—"

Daryn's smile because a fierce scowl. "You aren't my *daed*. Don't lecture me about being too young to get serious about a girl."

"I wasn't going to lecture you. Just advice, brother to brother."

"I don't need it! We're not serious. She and I are friends." He stabbed at a chunk of beef in the gravy as he added, "You know, you could use some friends, too, Mark."

"I've got Mattie and the Kuepfers."

"They're family and business partners. You need *friends*."

He forced a smile. "I will when I've got time for friends."

"Maybe you should make time. You should work on your people skills. From what I heard tonight, they're rusty."

"My meeting didn't have anything to do with people skills. It was business." He couldn't get Kirsten's voice out of his head. That was not *gut* because nobody must distract him from making the farm a success. Not even a pretty young woman with eyes flickering like summer lightning.

"Maybe so, but you'll never catch flies or anything else if you're confrontational. By the way, I'm heading out with friends tonight," he said as if he'd just thought of it, though Mark guessed the whole conversation had been leading to this point.

"Where?"

The wrong question because Daryn scraped up his last bite, stood and walked out of the kitchen.

Mark put down his fork. Leaning his forehead on the heels of his palms, he sighed. Tonight had gone from worse to worst. Kirsten would make sure his house was cleaned, and… He pushed the image of her smile from his head. She was so in control and competent.

As he wanted to be.

As he *had* been until Daryn became his responsibility.

"So, God," he whispered, "why isn't it as easy to find someone to help my brother see *gut* sense as it was to find someone to clean the house?"

Chapter Two

What a day!

Kirsten dragged her low spirits to the gate in the picket fence at her *aenti*'s house. The small, white farmhouse had a glorious view of the bay and its red sand beaches. It was a simple clapboard house, two stories with tall, narrow windows across the front. A porch wrapped around three sides, giving views of the bay and shelter from the wind. The paint was peeling on the windward sides, and she guessed repainting was something they'd have to do often in the harsh Prince Edward Island climate.

Like tonight when the icy breeze sliced into her bones, reminding her how many hours she'd worked at the Sea Gull Holiday Cottages before the humiliating meeting with Mark Yutzy.

Humiliation… That was something she was far too familiar with. She'd come to the Island in order to escape the embarrassment of knowing everyone was thinking about how she'd been the bride whose groom hadn't showed up for their wedding.

The enticing aroma of grilled burgers didn't ease her grim thoughts. *Aenti* Helga loved to cook outside, no matter the season. Weeks ago, the light breezes off the bay had been pleasant. Kirsten had been told, because of the Gulf Stream, the summer waters around the island were warmer than anywhere north of the Carolinas. She hadn't had a chance to dip her toe in the bay, because she'd been busy lining up clients for her cleaning company and working at Sea Gull Holiday Cottages.

Tonight, her boss, Lulu Wyler, had kept her late to talk about shutting down. Lulu had accepted reservations until the start of November because she wanted the extra income for a trip to Vancouver. By the end of the month, she intended to be there to hold her first *kinskind*, as she said several times with a smile, "before he's an hour old." In addition, she'd hinted the resort would be up for sale next year. Gail, the other housekeeper at the resort, had urged Kirsten not to worry.

"She's been saying that every year for a decade," Gail had reassured her as her broad smile rearranged the pattern of wrinkles on her tanned face. For years, Gail had worked on a fishing boat with her husband. When he retired, she hadn't been ready to give up working, so she'd gotten a job at the resort.

"She sounds serious," Kirsten had argued.

"She does at season's end. When spring comes around, she can't wait to get to work. Wait and see." After giving her a hug, Gail had headed to her home near the center of the small town of Shushan at the top of the bay.

Kirsten wished she could feel as sanguine about their futures at the cottages. Another layer of pressure had settled on her shoulders, a constant reminder of how much the family depended on her getting her business off the ground.

She would have been more optimistic if Mark Yutzy

hadn't complained when she thought her business was ready to become self-sustaining. Now, she had to deal with Janelle who would be more intense than Mark had been. When was the fifteen-year-old *not* intense? Janelle wouldn't be as reasonable as Mark. Any comment could send her into dramatics worthy of the greatest actor.

Kirsten paused by the gate and took a deep breath. If she came into the yard with her thoughts on her face, she'd upset her *aenti*. She released the breath as she looked around. She'd loved this spot as soon as she'd arrived. Tonight the water rippled on the red sand, but she'd seen it splash onto the road when a big storm boiled in the North Atlantic. Though the island was nestled into the curved arm of the Canadian Maritimes like a *boppli* cuddled in a *mamm*'s arms, it was not protected from storms. She'd heard islanders talk about past hurricanes and blizzards and how everything on the Island came to a stop while the wind howled.

Tonight, despite the penetrating breeze, was as perfect as a picture postcard. The glint of the moonlight danced on the bay, turning the water a rich silver. A few stars pierced the night sky, and within a couple of hours the glory of the Milky Way, something she'd never seen before she came east, would arch overhead like an invitation to explore eternity.

Stop it! She couldn't let her thoughts wander into fancy. Not after the uncomfortable meeting with Mark Yutzy. Again she wondered if she'd been *dumm* to agree to continue cleaning his house without speaking with Janelle first. Giving him a free cleaning? She must have been out of her mind.

She'd gone into the meeting annoyed. While she'd met with her boss, she'd stewed about the tone of Mark's note. Hadn't she learned letting her emotions get the best of her was stupid? She'd led with her heart too many times, and everything had gone wrong. On every step in the half mile between his farm and *Aenti* Helga's, she'd pondered how she could have handled that situation better.

As she walked into the house and through the empty living room to the dining room which was filled with a long table surrounded by benches and mismatched chairs, Kirsten jumped aside to avoid her twelve-year-old cousin Theo.

"I'm starving, and *Mamm* said we couldn't eat till you got home!" he shouted and bounced toward her, putting the plates he carried at risk. His reddish-brown hair caught the light from the overhead propane light.

"You're always starving, even when you've just finished eating." She ruffled his hair as she'd done since he was a toddler.

His reaction was the same as it'd been then. *"Duh sell net!"* His demand that she stop teasing him was ruined by how his eyes glistened with delight.

"You're the *boppli*, Theo," she retorted, delighting in the chance to play the game they enjoyed. "I get to tell you what to do."

"Not gonna listen."

"There is astonishing news," said his *mamm* as she came to rescue the plates. She wasn't as tall as Kirsten, but was larger boned. Her hair was the same color as her son's but laced with silver. Those graying strands hadn't been there before her husband's death. New wrinkles scored her face, too, hiding what once had been laugh lines. "You use your ears so seldom, Theodore, you wouldn't notice if they went missing."

As they laughed together, Kirsten pushed her worries about Mark Yutzy aside. She should be grateful that her other customers were satisfied.

Aenti Helga sent her son to get silverware while she took the burgers off the grill. After taking off her coat and bonnet and hanging them by the door, Kirsten gathered freshly baked rolls and containers of ketchup and mustard. Glancing around the kitchen with its white walls and pine cabinets and bright green counter, she saw no sign of her other cousin. She hurried into the small dining room which had faded flowery wallpaper. She put the items on the table before returning to get the macaroni and tuna salad as well as the applesauce *Aenti* Helga served with every meal.

After Theo put two large bottles of root beer on the table, *Aenti* Helga motioned for them to take their seats.

"Where's Janelle?" Kirsten asked as she sat beside Theo who gave her an eager grin. He would have dined on hamburgers or hot dogs or nachos every night.

"She went to visit a friend." *Aenti* Helga sat with a sigh that spoke of her fatigue. "She's young. She needs to have fun."

Kirsten wasn't sure how to reply. Janelle was fifteen, but in many ways acted younger than her brother. "Is she staying overnight?"

"No. She has the Martins' house to clean tomorrow morning, so I told her to be home by nine." Handing her son the ketchup, *Aenti* Helga sighed. "She wasn't happy, but Janelle isn't happy about much nowadays."

Theo's smile dimmed at those words, and Kirsten reminded herself how the first anniversary of *Onkel* Stanley's death was approaching fast. It would be the first week of February. She reached across the table and patted her *aenti*'s arm, hoping the motion would say what no words could.

Theo's spirits bounced back after they shared a silent prayer. He fixed his burger and took a big bite. He chattered about his day at school and shared every detail of the ball game at recess. He was prouder of getting on base three times than he was of the perfect score he received on his spelling test.

When he paused to concentrate on another burger, Kirsten asked her *aenti* about her day. It had been a light one. *Aenti* Helga had had only one house to clean instead of the two or three she did some days.

"I did the Carlisles' house today," *Aenti* Helga said. "You know, Dr. Carlisle and his wife, Michelle. He's the new veterinarian at Shushan Bay Animal Hospital."

Kirsten nodded. Two months ago, she'd gone to the animal hospital to ask if she could leave a flyer about her fledgling business. The receptionist had been new, so she'd had to ask Dr. Carlisle about their policy. The veterinarian had agreed to tack one of her flyers to his bulletin board and had arranged for her to meet his wife. Mrs. Carlisle had hired her within five minutes of her arrival. Pregnant with twins, Mrs. Carlisle asked for help unpacking the moving boxes piled throughout the house.

Kirsten had helped after work every day for the following week until the last box was empty. After giving the house a deep cleaning, she'd turned the job over to her *aenti*. Now *Aenti* Helga cleaned their house every week and gave Mrs. Carlisle basic cooking lessons as well as advice on raising *bopplin*.

It seemed to be a *gut* arrangement because her *aenti* looked forward to going to the house, and the Carlisles were pleased with how well *Aenti* Helga cleaned.

At least one client is happy. She silenced the thought and scolded herself. Why was she focusing on one unhappy client when she had a dozen who were pleased with Ocean Breezes Cleaning? When had she become so pessimistic?

When she'd found out her groom hadn't shown up for their wedding.

She'd gotten into the horrible habit of looking for a cloud around every silver lining. *Now the God of hope fill you with all joy and peace in believing, that ye may abound in hope...* So many times she'd prayed that verse from Romans 15:13, but her heart resisted its truth.

She tried again as she ate and listened to her *aenti* and Theo. She didn't like being glum and expecting something terrible. She wanted to return to the hopeful, upbeat person she'd been. Maybe it was impossible to believe in "once upon a times" after seeing that wasn't what God had in mind for her. She'd assumed she'd find the man of her dreams, marry and have a happy home filled with *kinder*. As her parents wanted her to do.

Kirsten was jarred out of her reproachful thoughts by her *aenti*'s laugh. Blinking as if waking from a nightmare, she heard *Aenti* Helga say, "You should see the stuff they have. Knickknacks everywhere and doilies. I've never seen so many doilies in so many different colors in one place in my whole life."

"Do they have a TV?" asked Theo.

Aenti Helga spread her arms wide. "This big, and another even bigger. Another one as big in each bedroom. Who needs that many televisions?"

"You shouldn't—" Kirsten began.

Her *aenti* paid her no mind as she continued to talk about the items she'd seen in the Carlisles' house. Most were items that wouldn't be found in a plain house.

Uneasiness burst into Kirsten's head as she heard the undeniable awe and envy in her *aenti*'s voice. Was *Aenti*

Helga considering leaving the Amish? That would be a monumental decision, because her *aenti* was a baptized member of the *Leit*. Leaving would mean being put under the *bann*. While she could live with her *kinder*, she couldn't share a table with them. Would Janelle and Theo leave, too?

Don't look for trouble, she told the dreary voice in her head. She'd seen no signs her *aenti* planned to jump the fence.

You didn't see when Loyal decided to live an Englisch *life,* argued her memories.

Loyal... What a joke that name had been! The first man she'd walked out with had joined a *rumspringa* group that was plain and *Englisch*. He'd tried to persuade her to join with him. If she had, would they still be together? Would he have expected her to leave her family behind as he had his?

Again she shoved aside her thoughts, but her impatience with those memories whetted her voice. "*Aenti* Helga, let's get dessert."

"I don't have—"

"Let's get it." She glanced from her *aenti* to Theo who was reaching for a third hamburger.

Aenti Helga frowned, but stood.

As soon as they were in the kitchen, her *aenti* asked, "What's wrong? I told you I didn't have time to make dessert."

"I wanted to talk without Theo hearing," Kirsten said.

"About what?"

"You shouldn't talk about what you see in clients' homes. They trust us to keep their personal lives private."

"I'm not talking about their personal lives, but, Kirsten,

you can't expect me not to be astounded. I've never imagined anyone would have as much makeup as—"

"No, *Aenti* Helga! You shouldn't—you can't talk like that. If someone overheard, they'd know what our clients had in their houses and where. A thief—"

Her *aenti*'s scowl deepened. "I was talking to you and my son. Neither of you is a thief."

"That's not the point. We've got to be careful about slipping into habits that could cause problems for our clients and for us."

"Us?" *Aenti* Helga's voice rose. "How could such casual talk cause us problems?"

"Because nobody's going to want to hire housekeepers who chatter about what they've seen and heard. The Carlisles have been *gut* clients, and I don't want to lose them."

"We're not going to lose them. You worry too much." Her *aenti* folded her arms in front of her, a sign she believed she'd had the final word.

Kirsten had learned how impossible it was to get her *aenti* to budge when she wore that stubborn frown. Would *Aenti* Helga heed her warning, or would she continue with her prattle? On one hand, her *aenti* was right. Talking with other family members didn't create a problem, but gossip was insidious. It popped out at the wrong times and with the wrong people.

While she lived under her *aenti*'s roof, she must curb her tongue. She might be *Aenti* Helga's boss, but she was grateful *Aenti* Helga and *Onkel* Stanley had allowed her to come to Prince Edward Island with them. She must not forget how much she owed them. She didn't have to see every day her parents' disappointment in their only *kind*. All her parents had asked of her was to marry and have *kinder*, and she'd failed.

Four times.

She wanted to caution her *aenti* not to let *hochmut* get in the way of *gut* sense, but she had to content herself with saying, "I appreciate you listening, *Aenti* Helga."

Her *aenti's* smile returned as if it'd never disappeared. "Always, Kirsten. We're partners in this, ain't so?"

She nodded, though Ocean Breezes Cleaning was Kirsten's company, and if it failed, it would be disastrous. She didn't want to think about her *aenti* having to sell the farm *Aenti* Helga and *Onkel* Stanley had been so excited about buying.

"Kirsten? Something else is bothering you. What is it?"

"I stopped at Mark Yutzy's house on the way home." She stared at her clasped hands. "He'd sent me a note saying he wanted to talk to me about how we're cleaning his house."

"I don't clean his house."

"No, Janelle does." She looked at her *aenti*.

Comprehension blossomed on *Aenti* Helga's face before her heavy brows lowered in a scowl. "I hope you told him Janelle is doing her best."

"I did, and I…"

A knock at the back door was followed by Theo's steps. He called, "You've got a caller, Kirsten! A guy!"

"Well, well…" Her *aenti's* face lit with a smile. "Isn't that unexpected news! Or is it expected?"

"Unexpected," she said as she went to the door. She didn't want another man asking if she'd walk out with him. Four had already asked before dumping her.

First, Loyal Derstine had decided he didn't want her or a plain life after he began hanging out with *Englisch* friends two months after she and he had started walking out together. He'd ended up leaving the Amish for a barista at the *kaffi* shop where he'd been spending his time and money.

She'd thought Hans Tweedt might be interested in her when he offered her a ride home from every singing for three months. He'd put her and everyone else in the rearview mirror when he got a job as an over-the-road trucker. Last she'd heard of him, he'd purchased a truck and was running shipments from Nova Scotia to Alberta.

Nolan Oatney had seen her as a matchmaker rather than someone to court. He'd used her as an excuse to spend time with her best friend, Gwendolyn. Six months later, he'd asked Gwendolyn to be his wife. That one hurt because Kirsten lost two people who'd mattered to her. She'd tried to reach out to her friend by letter, but hadn't gotten any response.

The worst had been Eldon Wheeler. He'd been eager to walk out with her. After he'd asked her to marry him, she'd made her parents happy by accepting. Eldon had acted happy, too, but, looking back, there had been warning signs she'd missed. Small things about how he'd changed the subject whenever she brought up their lives after the wedding. Larger ones, including how he'd disappeared for days at time in the weeks leading up to their wedding. Their whole courtship had been a series of lies.

She silenced the little voice inside her head as she reached the door. She didn't want to be reminded again—as if she could ever forget—how much a mess her life had been in Ontario.

Her eyes widened when she saw who stood on the front porch. "Mark!" she gasped before she could halt herself. "What are you doing here?"

Mark Yutzy stood at the edge of the crescent of light

coming from inside the house, his straw hat in his hands. His voice was calm, but she couldn't mistake the twinkle in his eyes when he replied, "I've come to apologize."

His words shocked Kirsten.

Mark hadn't intended that, but her wide eyes confirmed it. He didn't want their second meeting to be as confrontational as their first.

That's the word Daryn had used, a word that had stung more than Mark had guessed a word could. *Confrontational.* It wasn't a description he liked attached to him. A plain man was supposed to hold out a hand to build a bridge, not use dynamite to create a chasm. How many times had Mark's *daed* said that? Not enough, it was clear, because Mark had allowed his anxiety about the farm spill into his conversation with Kirsten.

As they stood eye to eye, he was amazed how intriguing it was to be able to look at a woman without stooping. He watched, intrigued, as she wiped her face clean of her thoughts.

His lips tipped in spite of his efforts to appear as collected as she did. What sort of game had she convinced him, without a single word, to play?

"Would you two like something to eat?" asked the older woman in the kitchen. *She* was Helga, the one who'd come to his house. She hadn't said she worked for the company instead of owning it. He'd assumed, and that had been his first mistake.

Then her words sank in. "Two?" He glanced over his shoulder to see his brother standing by the picket fence.

Daryn went to the back gate, pulled it open and walked toward the house.

"I thought you were out with friends," Mark said.

"I was." He stopped and stared at the grass beneath

his work boots. "I was walking past, and I didn't see you until you stepped into the light from the door."

"Uh-huh." He could tell when Daryn was lying. The teen never met his eyes when he was spinning a tale.

"Are you coming in?" asked Helga.

"I'd like—" Daryn began before Mark could answer. Footsteps approached along the road, and Daryn's eyes cut to a young woman ambling toward them.

As she came closer, she put up her hand to keep her *kapp* in place as a gust of wind rose off the bay. He recognized her as the girl who'd cleaned their house yesterday. Or at least attempted to...

"What's going on?" the girl asked. "You didn't tell me you were planning a party, *Mamm*."

If the girl was Helga's daughter, she was Kirsten's cousin. If he'd known they were related to Kirsten, he might have chosen different words to get his point across. It was a wonder Kirsten hadn't stormed out, insulted by how he belittled... What was her name? *Janelle.*

When Daryn stepped forward, grinning, Mark guessed his brother didn't have to remind himself of the girl's name. "We decided to visit you."

Janelle smiled.

Mark glanced toward Kirsten. Her eyes narrowed as she looked from Janelle to his brother.

"*Mamm*," Janelle said with a smile. "I know you've met Mark, but this is his brother, Daryn."

"Are you hungry?" Helga asked again as his *mamm* would have. No matter how much she'd had to struggle to feed her husband and *kinder*, she somehow found enough for guests.

"Are those burgers I smell?" asked Daryn.

"*Mamm* makes the juiciest burgers." Janelle motioned toward the dining room. "*Komm*, and try one."

As the two teens walked past her, Kirsten said, "I thought you were having supper when I stopped by."

"I told you. His stomach is a bottomless pit." Mark stepped inside. He paused when he saw his brother pulling out a chair at the table while introducing himself to the boy sitting there.

"Nice to meet you, Theo," Daryn was saying. "How are the burgers?"

"*Mamm* makes the best ones," the younger boy replied. "Go on. Try one."

"How about you, Mark?" Helga asked as she motioned for him to take a seat. There were two empty chairs, and he guessed Kirsten had been sitting on one.

"*Danki*," he replied, "but I try to limit myself to three meals a day."

The older woman laughed. "I'm waiting for when Theo can get by with only three. Cookies are gone as soon as they come out of the oven." She shot a glance at Kirsten, but either Kirsten didn't see it or chose to ignore it.

Mark saw it, though. Helga wanted Kirsten to insist he sit. No need. He had to keep an eye on Daryn who couldn't stop staring at Janelle. Did she know he'd be leaving for Ontario early next year? *Daed* planned to have Daryn learn more about running the factory since Mark had made it clear he wouldn't return if he could make a go with the farm.

Drawing in a deep breath, Helga released it. "How about something to drink? I've got *millich* or root beer. If you'd prefer *kaffi*, I can make—"

"Root beer?"

"*Ja.* I make a big batch every year. I sent a few bottles over with Janelle. Didn't she give it to you?"

"That was yours?" Mark asked and cut his eyes toward Daryn. "It was delicious."

Janelle said, "*Mamm* won't let us watch her make it, but she promises she'll teach me the secret recipe one of these days."

"Have you thought about selling it, Helga?" he asked.

Helga made a soft mewing sound and hurried toward the kitchen, leaving Kirsten and her cousins with bereft expressions.

"Did I say something wrong? I didn't—" Mark began. He was shocked into silence when Kirsten gripped his arm and tugged him away from the table. He had the bizarre thought she intended to take him out behind the shed for a thrashing. That thought was followed by the image of them alone and her stepping closer.

He dislodged both ridiculous images. He didn't have time for a relationship, most especially with a woman like Kirsten Petersheim who'd made it more than clear she didn't like him.

When she opened the front door and stepped onto the porch, he said, "If I said something wrong…"

"You did, but you didn't know. I don't want her to overhear us." Kirsten sighed. "The truth is *Aenti* Helga stopped making root beer after *Onkel* Stanley died."

"I'm sorry. If I'd known, I would have chosen my words with more care."

"There's no reason for you to apologize."

"I'm sorry. For you losing your *onkel* and for what happened at my house."

In the light flowing through the windows, he saw her brows lower in the same puzzled expression she'd worn when he came to the door. "You didn't do anything wrong."

"You're being nice, Kirsten, but if Theo had spoken to you as I did at my house, you would have reminded him of his manners."

"Most likely."

His respect for her rose another notch. She wasn't trying to play to his ego as other women had. He appreciated that. A lot.

"Daryn made a point of telling me I was a *dummkopf*," he said. "How could you and Janelle know what I wanted when I hadn't told you?"

"That's true. We aren't mind readers."

"It would make your job a lot easier if you were."

A faint smile tugged at her lips. "It would."

"I meant what I said about trying your service again."

"Danki."

When she didn't say anything else, he found he couldn't tear his gaze away from her pretty face. He'd never been able to look another woman straight in the eyes. This was a fascinating experience, and it gave him the chance to notice how fine wisps of her black hair curled in front of her ears and folded over the edges of her *kapp*. They accented the intriguing lines of her face, which were assertive and soft at the same time. She was a woman to be reckoned with, one who lived life on her and God's terms.

"*Komm* and get some root beer!" Helga's call rang from the dining room.

A jolt of something cut through him, and he saw Kirsten wince, too. Had she been caught up in the moment too?

As she turned to answer her *aenti*, he wanted to shake away the connection forming between them. He couldn't be distracted by pretty eyes when he must keep his own on his brother, so Daryn stayed out of trouble.

He'd been warned. He wouldn't be *dumm* enough to be alone with her in the moonlight again…or any other time.

Chapter Three

The following Friday, Mark raised his arm to wave goodbye to the truck driver, then winced. His shoulder recalled every time he'd lifted a shovel filled with potatoes and dropped them onto the conveyor into the truck. He tried not to think how many kilos he'd moved that day.

The bulk of his crop was on its way to Charlottetown where it would be made into fried potato products. He looked at the paper the driver had given him. It stated the company would pay him within thirty days. He smiled when his gaze focused on the amount. It would be more than enough to tide him over the winter and to buy seed in the spring. Maybe not enough to pay for fixing up the outbuildings, but he should be able to paint the interior of the house and clear out the smaller barns which were filled with tools and rusty equipment someone else might be able to use.

Near the small stacks of potatoes remaining in the dark, dank barn, Daryn leaned on his shovel. His head hung low, and Mark wondered if his youngest brother had ever worked so hard.

"*Danki* for your help," Mark said as he walked to

where his brother stood. "I'm about ready for a shower. How about you?"

The teenager raised his head and grinned. "More than you can know. How about something cold to drink first?"

"Sounds perfect."

When Daryn raced toward the house, Mark shook his head. *Lord*, he prayed with a grin, *if I could have half his energy and stamina again.*

Everything about farming had been harder than he'd expected, but he loved the challenge of making sure crops were planted at the right time—with enough weeks to ripen but not too early so a late frost would ruin them—and selecting the exact moment to harvest. He hadn't done everything right this year. Not by a long shot. His corn had gone in later than it should have, but the weather had cooperated and the ears had grown and ripened on schedule.

"Here you go," Daryn said, walking into the barn and holding out a glass. "The last of the root beer." He sighed. "Do you think Helga Petersheim would send more if we asked?"

Mark took a long drink of the brown fizziness, then wiped his lips with his hand. "You might offer to buy some."

"With what?" He mimed turning his pockets inside out. "All I've got is lint."

"With the potatoes—"

"*Ja*, I know," Daryn said in a tone perfect for a martyr...or a teenager. "With the potatoes sold, you'll pay me once you've been paid. Then I'll have money to burn."

"I hope you don't burn it."

"You know what I mean."

Mark clapped him on the shoulder. "I do, and I appreciate you agreeing to this arrangement."

"I didn't agree. *Mamm* and *Daed* did." He jerked away, his *gut* spirits vanishing as he hunched into himself.

"But you stayed."

"What was my other choice? Going home and having *Mamm* and *Daed* watch me like a wolf watches sheep? Waiting for me to make a mistake?"

"They want to protect you."

"What about learning from my mistakes? How can I do that if I'm never allowed to make one?"

"You're asking the wrong person. I'm not your *daed*. I'm your brother. Your sweaty brother." He smiled. "Do you want the shower first or me?"

"First." He hurried toward the house.

"Don't use all the hot water. Again!"

His brother's chuckle wafted to him.

Mark took another sip of the root beer. It was *gut*. Spicy, but not overly so. Enough to make a man sit up and take notice.

Like Kirsten Petersheim.

Whoa! Where had that thought come from? The pretty brunette had tried to pop up in his mind several times during the past week, but he'd squelched the thoughts.

"You're too tired to fight your brain," he mumbled.

He'd give his brother fifteen minutes for his shower. If the boy took a second longer, Mark would bang on the door in hopes of having at least a little hot water.

In the meantime, he'd make up three-kilo bags as well as four-and-half kilo bags for the family's store. He'd promised to deliver them to Mattie this morning. It was past noon, and he didn't want customers at the Celtic

Knoll Farm Shop to be disappointed if they were looking for potatoes. Mattie and her sister, Daisy, had worked
too hard to get the shop up and running for him to let
them down.

Driving his open wagon between the large Quonset
hut holding the family's farm shop and two smaller ones
that were little more than skeletons, Mark was pleased
to see four cars and an equal number of buggies in the
parking lot. Mattie and Daisy had a steady clientele.

The shop was set on a slight rise offering beautiful views of the bay and the cliffs that rose on the far
side. Late season mums clung to the walk to the front
door, adding bright splashes of yellow and orange. Bins
with apples and winter squash created a patchwork of
color beside a side door. The potato bins, he noticed,
were empty.

He parked by the wide doors to the rear storage room.
"Coming?" he asked as he swung down from the seat.

His brother grumbled, "Why? I won't have time to
look around before you make me unload the wagon."

"*Help* me unload the wagon. We're partners in this."

"We aren't partners. You're the boss, and I'm the in-
dentured servant."

Mark considered responding, but didn't. The last
time Daryn had whined like this, he'd called Mark
the jailer and himself the prisoner. The time before it
was guard for Mark and a member of a chain gang for
Daryn. There had been more Mark had forgotten. If
Daryn spent as much time working as he did in coming up with ridiculous comparisons, the job would have
been done already.

He remained silent and opened the door to the Quonset hut's storage room. Passing between the stacks of

boxes and bags waiting to be put on the shelves for customers, he halted when he saw a motion. He was greeted by a blonde teen who rolled her wheelchair toward him.

"How are you doing, Daisy?" he asked, bending to give her a hug.

"We're doing great." She squeezed him before holding up the battered doll she always had with her. "Boppi Lynn is happy to see you."

Smiling, he said, "I'm happy to see her. Where's Mattie?"

"With customers." Daisy pointed over her shoulder toward the door opening into the store. "Where else? Are you sure you want to talk to her? She's mad."

"At me?"

"*Ja.* Customers want potatoes, so Mattie wants potatoes. You bring potatoes."

Mark chuckled. He was glad Mattie had brought her younger sister with her to Prince Edward Island. Daisy's Down syndrome made her blunt. He appreciated that.

His *gut* humor vanished when he opened the door to the shop and stepped out. Nearly into a woman.

As he started to apologize, his words tumbled into each other like a stack of wooden blocks. He stared at Kirsten's shocked face. For the past week, he'd imagined seeing her again. Now he couldn't think of a single word to say without stuttering like a wet-behind-the-ears teenager asking a girl to let him drive her home for the first time.

Where had *that* come from?

Kirsten was surprised. Mark hadn't had trouble with words before. The opposite, in fact, because he'd aired his opinions the evening she went to his house to check on Janelle's work.

At the thought of her cousin, Kirsten glanced toward the front of the shop where Janelle was talking to Mattie Kuhns by the cash register. Janelle had pleaded with Kirsten to stop as they were driving past the Celtic Knoll Farm Shop and had jumped out of the buggy before it had rolled to a stop, leaving Kirsten and Theo to follow at a more rational rate. Theo had gone to talk to a boy close to his age who was tossing a ball in the air and catching it. Kirsten had entered the shop because she'd assumed Janelle wanted to buy something, but instead the teenager headed for Mattie. What was that about?

Mark was silent, so Kirsten said, "If I can get my cart past you…"

He jumped to the side as if she'd poked him with the cart. "Sorry."

She started to walk past him, but stopped when he spoke again.

"I'm sorry for running you down, too," he said.

This was ridiculous. She had no reason to worry about impressing him. Grasping for something to say, she fell back on business. "Janelle will be at your house as scheduled Wednesday."

"*Gut.*"

Again she waited for him to say more, but when he didn't, she pushed on the cart to go around him. He put out a hand to grab the front, shocking her.

And shocking him, because his pale brows shot upward as if he couldn't believe what he'd done.

He took a slow breath, then said, "I think we've gotten off on the wrong foot, Kirsten."

"You had every right to complain about Janelle's work."

"Can we move beyond that?"

"*Ja.* I'd like that."

"Me, too." His broad shoulders eased as he glanced into her cart. "Carrots, onions, peas. Are you making stew?"

"I was going to, but there aren't any potatoes."

"I can help with that. Wait here."

Before she could answer, he pushed through the door. He was back moments later with a bag of potatoes. Putting it in the cart, he said, "Fresh from the field."

"*Danki*. You didn't need to—"

"Trust me. If I let you go away without potatoes, I'll never hear the end of it. Mattie and Daisy want to keep their customers happy."

Kirsten relaxed, too, as she smiled. "I understand that."

Theo raced up to them along with a half-dozen other boys. "Mark! We're going to play baseball on the beach. Want to be on my team?"

"Sorry," he said. "Daryn and—"

"Daryn can play too."

Mark shook his head. "We've got to unload potatoes."

Theo's lower lip stuck out in a pout. "We wanted you to play with us."

"I've got an idea," Kirsten interjected when Mark looked taken aback by Theo's childish protest. "If you and your friends help Mark and Daryn unload the potatoes, they'll have some time to play ball with you. Would that work, Mark?"

She'd shocked him. She could tell by how his eyes widened. She was about to apologize for making assumptions when he said, "Sure. That's a *gut* plan."

"If the whole team helps," she said with a smile at the boys, "you and Daryn can play longer, Mark. Many hands make light work, ain't so?"

"We'll help." Theo was grinning again as he glanced over his shoulder. "Right, guys?"

The other boys agreed with varying degrees of enthusiasm, but Theo didn't seem to notice.

"If you want to help unload," Mark said with a wry smile in Kirsten's direction, "I'd be out of my mind to say no. I get your help, *and* Daryn and I get to play ball."

Theo started to cheer, but Kirsten hushed him as other customers peered in their direction. When she looked at Mark to thank him, he was appraising her as if for the first time. She was curious what he was thinking, but didn't ask.

"Can I catch?" Mark asked, astonishing her because she'd been sure his next words would be to ask why she'd volunteered him, without asking first, to join the game.

"You don't want to pitch?" Theo gasped, and the others exchanged baffled glances. "Everyone wants to pitch."

"Not me. I like to catch. I can observe the other teams' batters up close and signal the pitcher to help strike them out."

Theo pondered the idea, then grinned. "So will you be our catcher?"

"*Ja.* Once the potatoes are unloaded. *Komm mol.* Time's a-wastin'."

That brought laughter from her cousin. "You sound like an old man."

"Compared to you, I am. Time to work, so we can play."

Motioning for the other kids to follow, Theo hurried toward the side door.

"*Danki,*" Kirsten said as she looked at Mark and quickly away. She had to stop thinking anything she said would be considered flirting. Eldon had chided her for flirting with other men. She hadn't thought she was, but wondered if she knew what flirting was. Talking to a man shouldn't be flirting, ain't so?

"For what?"

"What you said was *wunderbaar*. Theo is often sad when other boys ask their *daeds* or older brothers to play. He misses his *daed*."

"I didn't think of that."

"No reason why you should." She smiled as she heard a thump from beyond the door. "You'd better go and rescue your potatoes before they end up pre-mashed."

"I'll make sure Theo gets home."

She couldn't help being touched by his thoughtfulness. "*Danki*, and you and Daryn are welcome to join us for supper."

"With Theo and Daryn there, maybe I should get you more potatoes."

Laughing, she started to reply, but halted when another thud was followed by a boy howling, "You dropped it on my toe!"

"No, I didn't," came a loud denial.

"You did. On purpose."

Mark threw open the door. As the door swung shut, she heard him trying to corral the boys in an effort to save his potatoes and their feet.

Kirsten grinned as she steered her cart to the register. Janelle stepped aside, clamping her lips closed.

"Everything okay?" Kirsten asked, curious why her cousin didn't want her to hear what she'd been discussing with Mattie.

"Everything's great," her cousin said.

Quelling her curiosity, Kirsten put her groceries on the counter and smiled at Mattie, whose hair was as pale a blond as her cousin's. Mattie totaled the items and bagged them. Kirsten was surprised when Janelle picked up the bags as soon as the transaction was done.

"Bye, Mattie!" she called.

"See you soon," Mattie answered before turning to her next customer.

Kirsten couldn't keep from glancing toward the back of the shop when she walked out behind her cousin. She smiled as she saw Theo, Daryn and the rest of the boys had formed what looked like a bucket brigade. Instead of water, they were passing potato bags along the line.

Setting the groceries in the buggy, Janelle got in. Kirsten did, too, and reached for the reins.

"Aren't you forgetting something?" Janelle asked.

"What?"

"Theo!"

Kirsten laughed as she turned the buggy toward the shore road. "He's staying to play ball with Mark and the boys."

"Oh." Janelle chewed on her lower lip, then said, "I saw you talking with Mark Yutzy."

"*Ja.* Theo and I did."

"Theo?" Shock stiffened her. "What was he talking to Mark about?"

"Playing ball."

Janelle sighed, and Kirsten asked her what was wrong.

"Nothing." Janelle hesitated. "Be careful with him, Kirsten."

"Him? Are you talking about your brother or Mark?"

"Mark! Haven't you heard what people say?"

"I don't listen to gossip."

"Maybe you should, because there's usually truth in it." Her voice dropped to a whisper.

"What truth?"

Janelle's voice grew softer. "I've heard he's one of

those men who doesn't care who's in his way, because all he can see are his goals. He pushes by everything else—and everyone." She sighed again, this time loudly. "Look whom I'm talking to! You know about men like that better than anyone else, ain't so?"

Kirsten forced herself to ease her grip on the reins before she hurt the horse's mouth. Janelle's words had been like a slap across the face.

But true.

She'd believed the men she'd walked out with were interested in her. She'd been wrong. Lloyd had wanted an *Englisch* life. Hans had wanted a truck. Nolan had wanted her best friend. What had Eldon wanted? Not her.

Janelle thought Mark was like Kirsten's four suitors, focused on what *he* wanted and not caring about her.

Kirsten couldn't let herself be attracted to another man who had more important matters on his mind than her. Hadn't she learned her lessons with Nolan, Loyal, Hans and Eldon? She'd told herself after each one she wouldn't be foolish again. Three times, she'd forgotten as soon as another man showed her attention and kindness. How many more times did she need to be taught God's plan for her didn't include a husband and a family? On her knees, she'd promised Him she'd heed His wishes and let the dream go.

This time, it was a promise she intended to keep for herself…and for her family.

Chapter Four

On Monday afternoon, Kirsten stood in her newest client's driveway, putting her cleaning supplies into her buggy. A gust of icy wind came off the bay, but unlike where she lived, this house was half-hidden behind guardian trees. The leaves and needles sifted the wind, diminishing its strength. She smiled as she looked at the small yellow house with its pine green shutters. The owner was Francis Wentworth, an elderly man who'd come to Prince Edward Island from the north of England and spoke with such a heavy accent she sometimes had trouble understanding him. He must have made an effort to pick up the clutter before she arrived to clean. She wasn't sure where he'd packed away the many items he moved, leaving outlines of where they'd been in the thick dust on his furniture. Though she appreciated his efforts, she'd find a way to let him know she didn't mind moving knickknacks and mementos while she worked. Seeing what her clients displayed gave her insight into them so she could do a better job for them.

It was important because she contributed everything she earned to her *aenti*'s family. When she'd first arrived to stay with her *onkel* and *aenti*, she'd been excited to discover they had a farm. Then *Onkel* Stanley had died. How many times had she prayed God would send her insight so she could help Theo who was determined to step in to take over from his *daed*?

She guessed, a year later, Theo didn't know much more than she did, though he'd gone to the local library to take out books to read about agriculture on the island. Reality hadn't popped his dream or his resolve, but a twelve-year-old boy couldn't handle planting and tending the fields by himself. Though he'd be thirteen next spring, as he reminded them at least a dozen times each day, he was too young to oversee a farm.

Kirsten believed they should rent out the land until Theo was finished with school in two years. When she'd spoken to *Aenti* Helga, the older woman had agreed but had wanted to wait until spring before discussing it with Theo. She feared announcing the plan would break his heart because he'd see that as confirmation they didn't believe in him. If his size matched his courage, he'd have been ten feet tall. He was a *kind*, and she, his *mamm* and his sister must find a way to keep his hopes alive at the same time they earned enough to feed themselves and pay the farm's mortgage.

Janelle had finished school in the spring and had been looking for a job, but hadn't found one while mired in grief. *Aenti* Helga had gotten a job babysitting quickly and then lost it as fast. Her *aenti* hadn't wanted to talk about what happened.

Aenti Helga and her *kinder* were dependent upon Kirsten's small paycheck, so she couldn't think of going home, though she could have used a large dose of the laughter that filled her family's house. The idea of Christmas without her parents was harder to face as the holiday approached. She'd considered going back to

Ontario for a few days, but her cleaning clients wanted more service around the holiday than usual.

Or was she just using that as an excuse to stay in Prince Edward Island? Here she didn't have to think about her four failed relationships, yet they loitered around the corners of her mind, pouncing whenever she let down her guard. It was as if each disastrous courtship was happening again, and each time, Kirsten was on the losing end.

Enough! she chided herself. Living in the past was useless. Move forward. That was her new motto.

Kirsten stretched to store the furniture polish in its box at the rear of the buggy, then yelped and jerked her hand back. It was too late. A splinter had been driven into the index finger on her right hand. Pain seared from it. She dropped the plastic bottle she held. It bounced and rolled across the frozen ground. She ignored it as she tried to pluck out the splinter, being careful not to break off the tiny point poking from her skin.

"Do you need help?"

At the deep voice, Kirsten spun so quickly she slipped on a patch of ice left from the cold rain last night. Broad hands reached out to steady her, but she sidestepped them, making sure she kept her footing on the slippery asphalt.

"*Danki*, but no," she said as she faced Mark who held out the bottle she'd dropped. It wasn't difficult to smile because she enjoyed looking at him. Taking the bottle, she warned herself again not to be attracted to another man obsessed with his goals. "I'm used to getting my supplies in and out of the buggy." She set the bottle in its proper place, then wiped her hands against each other, trying not to wince as she brushed her finger.

"What are you doing here…today?" She added the last word because the question seemed too rude otherwise.

He returned her smile. "I had errands to run in town for a project I'm working on."

She almost asked what his project was, then wondered if she would understand his answer. She hadn't grown up on a farm. Her *daed* oversaw a small shop behind their house. He took apart *Englisch* hand power tools and small appliances. After removing the electrical wires and controls, he rebuilt them to work on batteries or compressed air.

"Is your project going well?" she asked.

"As well as can be expected." He glanced at his dark trousers, and she noticed for the first time they were covered with small specks of white and brown. "I've been scraping paint off the living room molding. So far, I've found six different colors. I'll have the mess cleaned it up before Janelle comes back to clean next time."

"She'll work around your work. That's one thing we have to learn as house cleaners. We clean around other people's lives. Let me know if Janelle's work isn't to your satisfaction."

"I'm sure she'll do fine."

She blinked, amazed at his easygoing words. He'd been emphatic about his expectations when he called her to his house to complain about the bad job her cousin had done last week. Now he acted as if getting his house cleaned was the last thing on his mind.

Maybe it was.

His hands were clenching and unclenching at his sides. Was he intending to say something difficult? Should she tell him to spit it out?

Before she could decide, he asked, "What's in your buggy?"

He stepped forward to examine the wooden boxes she'd installed in the rear. The shorter ones held her jugs of cleaning liquids and scouring powders so they didn't move around when she drove from one job to the next. Boxes on their sides and stretching beneath the rear seat gave her storage for brooms and mops. Two bags hung from hooks on either side of the interior, one for her clean cloths and the other for soiled ones.

"These containers are clever," Mark said. "Did you build them yourself?"

"I did." She tried to submerge the *hochmut* stirring inside her heart as she thought of the time she'd put into measuring wood, cutting it and hammering the boxes together. Being proud of her simple creation was silly. God had given her the inspiration and guided her hands to build it.

His brow furrowed. "Aren't you getting a lot of slivers off that raw wood?"

"A few." She winced as she thought of the splinter in her finger. "I usually wear my rubber gloves when I'm taking things in and out, but I was in a hurry so I won't be late for my next job." Would he take that as a hint to let her get on her way?

He didn't. "I'd be glad to smooth down the sides for you." He pulled a package of sandpaper out of his pocket. Her surprise must have been displayed on her face, because he added, "Like I said, I was working on the molding at home."

"I don't think I've ever known anyone else who keeps sandpaper in his pocket."

"I was raised among stacks of wood in my *daed*'s woodworking shop. My *mamm* says I had a hammer in my hand along with a teething biscuit." He gave her a quick grin. "Getting more sandpaper was the reason

I went to the hardware store. Sanding the boxes won't take me long, and you won't have to worry about getting splinters."

"In that case, *danki*." Why was she being skittish around Mark? It wasn't as if he'd shown interest in her. Not like other guys had when they pursued her…until they found someone or something else they were more eager to have.

"If you'll remove your supplies…"

"You want to sand the boxes now?"

"No sense in you getting a sliver, ain't so?" He frowned as her gaze slid to her throbbing finger. Without asking her permission, he lifted her hand as cautiously as if it were made of milkweed floss. "Guess I'm too late. It's in deep, ain't so?"

"Ja." Were her fingers trembling, or were his as he bent toward her?

"Don't move."

"What?"

He pinched the sore spot on her index finger, then raised his head, grinning. "Got it." He held up a teeny piece of wood.

She was amazed. The sliver had felt as big as a log. *"Danki.* I thought I was going to have to wait until I could get home and use a needle and tweezers."

"You can't work in a woodworking shop for long without becoming skilled at dealing with splinters." He laughed as he released her hand.

Something sharp pierced her. Not a splinter this time, but a sense of regret he wasn't holding her hand any longer.

Was she out of her mind? Four men had been eager to hold her hand, and she'd been thrilled to have them do so. Then each of them had dropped her hand and walked away.

"Danki," she said again.

She realized how clipped that single word had been when Mark's easy smile faded. Biting back an explanation before it could slip past her lips, she began lifting her supplies out of the boxes, so he could sand the wood.

"Let me," he said, his tone emotionless as he motioned her aside. He pulled a pair of work gloves from the same pocket where he'd had the sandpaper. "No need for you to get another sliver."

"Mark…"

"Hmmm?" He set her supplies on the driveway, being careful to avoid icy spots and puddles. Once he was done, he began scraping the sandpaper over the edges of the box he'd cleared out. Dust rose around his fingers.

As she watched the rough edges vanish beneath his steady motions, she said, "I should have done this long ago."

"Ja, you should have." He glanced up at her, and his smile reappeared, flowing upward from his lips to his eyes.

As he concentrated on the boxes, emptying each out by handing her what was stored inside and then rubbing the sandpaper along the wood, she was startled every time their fingers brushed. It felt as if she'd grabbed onto a lightning bolt.

More quickly than she expected, he said, "That should do it. If you want my advice, next time sand the wood before you put your boxes together."

"I will. *Danki* for the *gut* advice." She slid the last of her long-handled tools into the box under the seat. "I owe you one."

He reached for the buggy's rear flap before she could and lowered it, snapping it into place. "I'm glad to hear you say that." He faced her. "I stopped because I wanted to ask you a favor."

"If you want Janelle to come a different day, I'm sure—"

"No, nothing like that. It doesn't have anything to do with cleaning the house."

Growing more puzzled, she asked, "Then what are you talking about?"

When he hesitated, as if to formulate an answer, she was surprised. She wasn't accustomed to dealing with men who didn't seem to know what they wanted. Each of the four men she'd walked out with had possessed clear goals and went after them...without her.

Shaking those thoughts out of her head, Kirsten focused on Mark. She shouldn't be comparing him to her erstwhile suitors. It wasn't as if she were in love with Mark. Or like. He was prickly and as dangerous to her equilibrium as the splinters he'd sanded away.

"It's Daryn," he said, letting her escape her mishmash of thoughts.

"What about him?" Not giving him a chance to answer, she said, "You should tell him that Theo has been talking of nothing but how much fun he had playing baseball with you and Daryn and the other kids on the beach."

"That's what I wanted to talk to you about."

"The baseball game?"

He shook his head, and his pale hair wafted around his head like a golden fog. "Not the game, but how you handled the boys."

"I don't understand."

Leaning one hand on the buggy, he tried to smile. It matched his feigned pose of nonchalance. "Kirsten, you made those boys *want* to work. With a few words, you had them eager to help with unloading the potatoes. It was like watching Tom Sawyer convince kids to whitewash the fence. You somehow convinced them to do what they didn't want to do."

She chuckled. "It's what works with Theo. Giving him a reward guarantees a job well done."

"You knew what to do. I can't figure it out."

"I learned from my parents. Though they believed a job well done was a reward in itself, they gave me work I could do and a cookie when I was finished. I was willing to do about anything for one of my *mamm*'s chocolate oatmeal cookies." She laughed again, hoping it covered her abrupt dismay. It'd been so simple to meet her parents' expectations when she was young, but she hadn't been able to meet what they'd have considered most important—Kirsten finding a man to marry and having a household full of *kinder*.

"I wish cookies would work with Daryn."

"What worked for you when you were a kid?"

Color flashed up his face, softening its sharp angles. "I was a weird kid. I liked to work. A lot."

"You still do."

He pushed himself away from the buggy and straightened. "I like a challenge, but my brother doesn't. In fact, he doesn't react to anything the same way I did when I was his age."

His frustration was so palpable that she was surprised she couldn't see it hanging like a cloud between them. "You are two very different people."

"Very, very different. Can you help me learn to handle Daryn as well as you do Theo?"

"I don't know if *handle* is the right word. I try to guide Theo to make *gut* decisions."

"Whatever you call it, you're *gut* with *guiding* your

cousins. I get the feeling they *komm* to you with their problems instead of your *aenti*."

"They're teenagers, and there are plenty of things they feel they have to figure out as well as mistakes they don't want everyone to know about." She sighed. "But you're right. They don't go to their *mamm*. *Aenti* Helga is in mourning, so they don't want to add to her burden." She walked to the front of her buggy. She was going to be late if she didn't leave right away. "They're still in mourning themselves."

"Along with you."

"I miss *Onkel* Stanley. That's for sure, but he was their husband and *daed*. If there's anything I can do to ease their lives—even a little bit—I want to do it." She gave him a regretful smile. "Mark, I've got to go. I can't be late for my next job."

"I understand, but you didn't answer my question."

"I did. You're going to have to learn through trial and error what works for your brother."

He sighed and shook his head. "I tried that. Nothing has worked. I've been hoping things would improve, but they haven't. In some ways, they've gotten worse."

Kirsten should go, but leaving Mark by the side of the road seemed cruel when he was lost within his quandary, unable to find his way out. *Give to him that asketh thee.* The verse from Matthew whispered through her head.

Hoping her next client wouldn't be upset if she were a few minutes late, she asked, "Gotten worse in what ways?"

"Let me give you an example from earlier today. I went to get peanut butter to make myself a sandwich, and there wasn't any."

Were all his anxieties so inconsequential? "I can't

tell you how many times that's happened to me when I forgot to buy some."

"That's the point. I didn't forget to buy it. I'm sure I bought a new jar at the farm shop. I remember picking peanut butter off the shelf because I was jesting with my cousin Daisy about having her play ball with the kids next time. I remember talking with Mattie while I paid, and I remember putting the jar in my shopping bag. When I asked Daryn if he'd seen the new jar, he acted as if I were accusing him of a hideous crime."

"You think he's lying to you?"

"I don't think he's being honest. One thing you may not know, Kirsten. Daryn was on the brink of getting into serious trouble in Ontario. His running around gang included kids who'd already gained a reputation for mischief."

"What sort?"

"Nothing too serious. A gate left open in the fence, a bale of hay lit on fire in the middle of a field where it couldn't endanger anything else, buggy racing. That sort of thing. That's why our parents sent him to me. They hoped being away from those friends might stop him from getting in trouble."

She comprehended what he hadn't said. "You don't want to fail your brother, ain't so?"

It was a loaded question, at least in Mark's estimation. How could he explain how important success was to him? How had Kirsten gauged the truth?

He must be overreacting. It shouldn't have been an unexpected question after what he'd asked her. Maybe he should step aside and let her leave as she wanted to do.

That wouldn't help solve his dilemma. He'd discovered the answer yesterday at the farm shop…if he could persuade her to help him. He didn't have much time, he could tell, because she had her hand on the buggy door, eager to be on her way. Would he have another chance to seek her help? He wasn't sure, and he didn't want to let his chance slip through his fingers.

So he chose the easy route and, taking his hat off, he slapped it against his leg for emphasis as he said, "You're right. I want to make sure Daryn does the right thing and stays out of trouble."

"That's not what I asked. Oh, never mind," she said, waving aside his response before he could speak. "I'm not sure I'm the right person for you to ask."

"You're doing a great job with your cousins."

"I'm glad you think so. Theo is a *gut* kid. In fact, he may be trying to be too *gut*."

"What do you mean?"

She sighed as her gaze slid away from his. Why was she trying to avoid his eyes? He understood when he heard a hint of guilt in her answer.

"Before he died, my *onkel* asked Theo to step in as the man of the family, and Theo is trying. He's got school and chores, and he offers to take on more. I had to insist he not work for me."

"How did you convince him to change his mind?"

"By saying something I shouldn't have."

"That you didn't think he could handle the extra load?"

She shook her head. "No, I told him his *mamm* needed him more than I do. It was the wrong thing to say."

"Because you left him thinking he must assume all his *daed*'s chores?"

"I think that's what he heard." She sighed and looked

up at him again. "Now you see why I'm not the person to help you."

"I've got to admit I'd be thrilled if Daryn was conscientious like Theo."

Again she shook her head. "No, you wouldn't. We've got two sides of the same problem. Can't you see that? They must be *kinder* at the same time they take on responsibilities."

"Daryn isn't a *kind*. He's sixteen."

He was upsetting her. He could tell when he noticed how her lips drew into a straight line. Should he tell her that, if she had doubts about her ability to help him and Daryn, he didn't?

"Sixteen is an age when kids aren't *kinder,* but aren't adults," she said. "Janelle is fifteen and definitely a work in progress."

"Sounds like Daryn."

"Don't you remember what it was like when you were their age?"

He ran his hand through his hair, then realized he'd left it standing straight up. He almost patted it down, but didn't want Kirsten to think he was vain. Instead, he put his hat on.

"I was working in my family's shop when I was his age," he replied. "I worked long hours, so I didn't have much time to fool around." He grimaced. "I've already seen that's not the solution with Daryn. I can't get him to help around the farm more than six hours a day. He's always got an excuse. Some are bizarre, but he tells me each one is true."

"I see."

He yearned to demand she explain what she seemed to understand when he remained baffled. "Does that mean you'll help me?"

"I'll try."

"Gut."

"You have to be part of this, too, because you're going to be part of the solution."

"Me? I can't get through to him. Asking a simple question like had he seen the jar of peanut butter seems to set him off. He doesn't want to listen to a single thing I say."

"That's because you haven't said anything he feels is important enough to heed."

He frowned. This was not going as he'd prayed it would. "I talk to him about the farm, about the house, about—"

"Chores."

"Ja. There are plenty of them."

She shook her head. "That's the wrong approach. Work is a bone of contention between you. Find common ground about other things. What does he like to talk about?"

"I'm not sure."

She rolled her eyes and asked, "Do you ever actually listen to each other?"

He almost chuckled. The motion that annoyed him to distraction with his brother was adorable when Kirsten did it.

"What's Daryn interested in?" Before he could answer, she went on, "Sports?"

"Probably."

"Food?"

"Always. As you've seen for yourself, the boy must have a hollow leg."

"Girls?"

He gave her a wry grin. "Most definitely, but that's a subject he's not going to want to talk about. At least

with me. I think there are a few girls he'd like to ask
to take home from a youth event, but I've got no idea
which ones."

"Maybe all of them."

"True. At sixteen, everyone is so nervous if a girl
looks at a boy, they start to believe they're committing
to a lifetime relationship."

Did Kirsten flinch? Why? What about his jest had
upset her?

Before he could ask, she said, "You've got to talk
about things he's interested in. Things that aren't on
your to-do chores list."

"All right."

"Gut." She swung up into the buggy and took the
reins. "Let me know how it goes."

Mark found he was saying, *"Danki,"* to the back of
her buggy as she drove out of the drive and along the
road.

He went in the opposite direction on the deserted
road following the curve of the bay. Ducking his head
into the wind that was growing colder as the afternoon
unfolded, he asked himself if the answer to his problems with his brother could be that simple?

The right solution is the simplest one.

Daed was fond of that saying. Kirsten had told him
the same.

He was about a kilometer along the road when he
stopped and stared at a boat pulled up next to the shore.
Greeley MacDonald, an *Englischer* who supplied fish
for the farm shop, moored his boat in that small inlet.
The fisherman's house was across the road, though
house was a generous description of the tiny building
without a hint of paint on its weathered clapboards.

Mark frowned as he peered at the side of the boat.

Red lines slashed across it. What had happened here? Striding through the dried grass, he realized words had been written on the side in bright red paint.

"Fish stink," he read aloud as he walked around to the other side. "Fishermen stink more."

"Get out!" shouted a furious voice. A tall, thin man rounded the boat. Greeley's scowl eased as he said, "Mark! Sorry. I didn't realize it was you."

Mark pointed toward the boat. "Did you see who did this?"

"No, but if I find out, they're going to be sorry they spent their money on spray paint." He rubbed his grizzled chin. "I'll hand them over to the cops, and they can think about their artwork while they're sitting in a jail cell."

"Probably kids."

"Kids who should know better than to deface someone else's property." His face hardened again. "They'll be sorry if I catch them. They may think I don't know who did this, but I do."

Mark nodded, trying not to show how his stomach was roiling. He was afraid he might know who was involved, too. Though he prayed he was wrong, he prayed harder the hand on the spray can hadn't belonged to his brother.

Chapter Five

As everyone in the living room rose to begin their final song the next Sunday morning, Mark wished he could feel the peace and grace he used to experience at the end of a church Sunday service. That serenity had vanished around the time his brother had moved onto the farm.

He glanced at where Daryn stood beside Theo Petersheim. The two boys had spent a lot of time together during the past week, but Mark hadn't seen any change in his brother. Daryn wasn't making an effort to hide the fact he wished he could be anywhere other than church at Hosea Thacker's house. Their elderly neighbor, a carpenter, had spent the three-hour-long service sitting in a folding chair while Daryn scowled as he had since Mark had insisted he get out of bed.

Dragging Daryn out of bed had become a daily task, and Mark was tired of having pillows or shoes thrown at him when he came in to rouse his brother to start the day. He'd tried using the handle of a broom to bang against the floor beneath Daryn's bed, but that hadn't worked, so he'd trudged up the stairs and learned to duck behind the door as soon as he opened it and called out his brother's name.

As the service was coming to an end, Daryn struggled to stay awake. Next to him, Theo was singing as if he wanted to make sure his was the loudest voice in the room. Daryn appeared as if he were mouthing the words as he contorted his face to keep from yawning. He failed, and the yawn escaped. When the younger boy regarded him with awe, a coldness sank through Mark.

Had he made a huge mistake asking Kirsten to help him with Daryn? Mark hadn't thought until this morning about the consequences of bringing the two boys together. Though he prayed the kindness and respect the Petersheim family showed each other would rub off on Daryn, he should have realized his brother's insolent ways might appeal to Theo.

He'd hoped to make his life simpler. Not make Kirsten's more difficult.

As he thought of her, his gaze slid toward the women standing by the benches facing the men and settled on Kirsten who was between her *aenti* and her cousin. Janelle was also stifling a yawn, clamping her mouth closed when Helga looked in her direction.

Kirsten already had responsibility for a family and a brand-new business. He'd dumped his problems on top of that. He had to apologize the first chance he had and admit his error. No doubt, she'd be relieved to have one less thing to do.

What am I going to do with Daryn then? The half prayer, half desperate cry for help exploded from his heart. The annoyance he didn't want to feel crept through him as he wondered why his parents had to pass their problem on to him as he was beginning to move forward with the farm.

He pushed away the irritation. His parents had sent Daryn to him because Mark had solved problems for the family before, and they hoped he could do the same with their youngest son. He was left without a solution and nowhere to turn.

Ask Kirsten. She'll help.

There had to be another solution.

But what?

Wishing he could escape from his thoughts that were going in endless, unproductive circles, Mark went through the motions of setting up the space in the house's living room for the meal served after worship was complete. He watched Kirsten as she worked with the other women to serve sandwiches along with chips and pickles.

"She's easy on the eyes, ain't so?" The loud question was followed by a wheezy laugh.

He turned to see their host. Hosea Thacker was a wisp of a man. Maybe in his prime, his shoulders had been broader and his legs less bandy, but the old man in front of him reminded Mark of a bird. His hair was the same white shade as a snow goose's feathers. He was as spry as a robin, and his voice carried like a crow's.

A quick scan of the room let Mark give a silent sigh of relief. Nobody else seemed to be reacting to Hosea's question. He shouldn't either.

"I'm glad you came over," Mark said. "I wanted to talk to you about some work I'm doing at my house." He gestured toward the moveable wall that had been pushed aside to make the living and dining rooms into one open space large enough for the *Leit* on a Sunday. "I'm taking out a wall in my house, and it's a support wall, so a beam will have to be installed. I've never done that."

"I can stop by later this week, if you'd like."

"There's no hurry."

"That's *gut* to hear because not hurrying is my favorite speed these days." Hosea gave him a hearty clap on the arm. As he turned toward the table and the plates stacked with sandwiches, he paused. "Don't think that I didn't notice how you avoided answering my question."

Mark had to smile as the old man toddled away on his bowed legs. Hosea was right, but talking about how pretty Kirsten was when so many ears could listen would be foolish.

For the first time, as he grabbed his coat and straw hat and went out the door, he felt a true hint of regret that he didn't have time to spend with such a lovely woman. He'd been dismayed in Ontario when young men in the shop had talked about the gals they were interested in walking out with. Being noncommittal had worked for him, and he'd been so focused on manufacturing quotas and quality control, the other guys didn't question him further. It'd worked fine then.

Now...

"Focus." He strode across the yard and away from the house.

The woodworking shop hadn't been his dream, but the farm was. Not making a go of it was the worst thing he could imagine. After planting next spring, Daryn was scheduled to return to Ontario. Their parents hoped that a year away from his troublemaking friends would be long enough to disconnect Daryn from the group.

He sighed. No matter how annoying his brother was, most of the time, he put in a fair day's work. Without Daryn to help, Mark wasn't sure how he'd harvest his potatoes next year. He'd have to plant extra acreage so he could hire help.

Mark stepped off the road and onto the beach, amazed as he was each time he saw the expanse of red sand. He leaned against a big boulder and watched the rhythm of the waves lapping over the crust of ice along the shore. There was something comforting in the unchanging motion.

Movement farther up the beach caught his eye, and he squinted to make out who else was out on the chilly afternoon. Kids, he guessed by their height and the faint chirping of their voices that were pitched too high to belong to adults. He couldn't tell if they were plain or *Englischers*. It didn't matter because they turned and walked in the direction from which they'd been coming.

Suddenly he was more aware of the cold than he'd been. And how the answer he sought wasn't going to come when he was distracted by the smallest thing, like a bunch of kids farther up the beach. He pushed away from the rock. Only as he took a step toward the house did he realize something was stuck to his shoe. Bending, he picked up a hand-knit black glove. There were splatters of red on the thumb. Something red and tacky, which was why it'd latched onto his shoe.

The red was the same shade as what had been used by the vandals on Greeley's boat.

"Don't jump to conclusions," he warned himself. There were plenty of red barns scattered along the bay. Many of them needed painting, and someone could have touched up a spot before winter.

But why throw away a *gut* glove?

"Someone could have dropped it." His words disturbed a flock of gulls, and they flew up with raucous cries.

As he watched them land on the open water in the center of the bay, he noticed another glove by a larger rock near where the birds had been gathered. He walked over and discovered it wasn't a single glove, but two. Both for the left hand, but only one had paint on it. Did that mean one of those who'd painted the graffiti on the boat was left-handed? How many people on the Island had a dominant left side? Too many to narrow down the search.

Assuming these gloves had anything to do with the graffiti. He couldn't even be certain of that.

Yet it was easy to imagine the kids standing on the beach and tossing the gloves into the bay. They'd assume the clue to their crime would be swept out to sea.

He should take the gloves to Greeley. The *Englischer* might recognize them, though that was unlikely. Mark had seen identical gloves available for sale in the hardware store in Shushan as well as in several other shops. He had a pair himself.

So did Daryn.

His stomach cramped at the thought. He balanced the gloves in his hand before stuffing them into his coat pocket until he could talk to Daryn about the vandalism.

If his brother had played a part in it…

Mark gritted his teeth, determined not to jump to conclusions. He wished he could discuss this with Kirsten. How did she confront difficult issues with her younger cousins?

As he neared the house, Mark heard happy shouts from the far side of the barn. He walked to where he could see what was happening. A baseball game. He should have expected that. Kids played ball—either baseball or soccer—from mud season until snow made it impossible to run. He'd been like that when he was a kid, too. Sitting through a long church service was bearable if he could throw or kick a ball around after the *Leit* shared their Sabbath meal.

How simple life had been! He thought of the black gloves in his pocket. If Daryn…

His eyes widened. What was Daryn doing the midst

of the *kinder*? His brother was nearly a head taller than the biggest kid. Daryn was grinning and talking eagerly to the youngsters gathered around him. Was this the same brother who'd thrown a hissy fit about getting up for church this morning?

"He's a natural with *kinder*." Kirsten came to stand beside him, her black wool coat buttoned up under her bonnet of the same color. A bright red scarf was wrapped under her collar, matching the shade of her wind-burnished cheeks. She was carrying a big platter of cookies.

His stomach did a few jumping jacks as his gaze swept over her pretty face. Why did the sun seem to shine more brightly and the wind blow less cold when Kirsten spoke to him? He'd never believed the romantic humbug his friends had gone on and on about.

So how did he explain his feelings?

He saw she was waiting for him to answer. As he took the platter to cover his pause, he asked the first thing that came into his head that wasn't about how her eyes twinkled like daylight stars. "How did you talk Daryn into playing with the younger kids?"

"I didn't." She clapped as one of the youngest ballplayers hit the ball, more by accident than design. "He offered."

Mark was so startled that he blurted, "He told me he wasn't going to babysit the little kids after church."

"He must have changed his mind." She gave a half turn to face him. "Have you always thought the worst of him, Mark?"

"I don't think…" He didn't continue as she bent to give a high five to the little girl who'd hit the ball and run the bases albeit in the wrong direction with Daryn keeping pace with her and pretending to trip as the kids roared with laughter.

This was his chance to ask her advice again about his brother. The words stuck in his mouth. He didn't want her to think he was worthless when it came to dealing with a teenager. He didn't want to think about why. That was dangerous territory to tread.

Very dangerous.

Something was bothering Mark.

Kirsten knew that as well as she knew her own name. Questions wafted through her head like an explosion of soap bubbles, but she didn't ask any. She'd learned one thing about Mark. He'd speak about whatever was bothering him when he felt the time was right.

The kids rushed over, and she took the plate back so she could hold it out to each one. Urging them to take two cookies, she smiled.

Where was Theo?

She fought to keep her smile in place. It wasn't like her cousin to skip playing ball or not be around for a sweet treat. The last time she'd seen him, he'd been talking with *Aenti* Helga who'd given a reluctant nod before he rushed out. Where had he gone?

When Daryn reached for a cookie, Kirsten's smile became more sincere. "It's nice of you to play with the little ones," she said.

"They're fun." Daryn grinned. "And funny."

"They thought *you* were funny when you acted as if you were going to fall on every step."

"I wasn't pretending." His mouth worked, and a laugh burst out. "Okay, I was, but I don't want the *kinder* to know. They think I'm a big goof so they feel comfortable around me."

"How did you figure that out?"

"I watched my big brother."

"Me?" asked Mark, unable to hide his astonishment. "I don't remember ever tripping over every base after hitting a home run."

"You didn't." Daryn took a big bite of the cookie, then reached for two more. "That's the point. You did everything right, so to make the kids laugh, I do the opposite." Waving the cookies at them, he loped away to join the youngsters.

Kirsten walked in the opposite direction to return the platter to the kitchen. When Mark fell into step beside her, she said, "Daryn is having a great time. It's *wunderbaar* to see him enjoying himself, ain't so?"

His smile vanished. Had her commonplace question touched a raw nerve? But why?

As if she'd asked that question aloud, Mark said, "As long as he's enjoying himself doing something positive."

"You must be glad to see him with a smile on his face."

"I am." He waited as she went to where *Aenti* Helga stood in the kitchen door.

When her *aenti* held out her hand for the plate, Kirsten asked, "Have you seen Theo? He wasn't playing ball with the other kids."

"He wanted to spend time with the boys he met after school on Friday." Lines dug into her brow. "I've told him to bring the boys to the house so I can meet them. They aren't from this district, and I think some are *Englischers*."

"When is he bringing them by?"

Her *aenti* shrugged. "I'm not sure." She looked past Kirsten. "Your young man is waiting. You'd better get going."

Kirsten didn't want to argue that Mark was not *her* young man. She was aware of other ears that might be listening. Explaining why she didn't want to walk out with anyone would mean reliving her past. That would bring her shame to the forefront again.

Hurrying down the steps, she didn't pause. She wasn't sure if she was glad or upset when Mark walked with her away from the house. Having him with her was a way to start gossip, but at least it wouldn't be about "poor, abandoned Kirsten, left again, this time on her wedding day."

"Everything okay?" Mark asked.

"*Aenti* Helga is worried about Theo and his new friends. She hasn't met them yet."

"I know how she feels."

"Daryn has friends you don't know?"

"*Ja*, and I want to be certain he's doing the right things instead of getting into trouble."

They continued walking toward the road. She side-stepped when one of the *kinder* came rushing toward them, chasing a ball. Scooping it up, she handed it to the little boy. He gave her a picket-fence grin. Wide gaps revealed where his baby teeth had fallen out and the new ones weren't in yet.

As he raced to the game, Kirsten said, "I'm planning to talk to Theo. Maybe he'll be more forthcoming about his friends with me than he is with his *mamm*."

"Don't count on it."

"Theo's been pretty open with me." She slowed as they paused to let a car and a buggy pass along the otherwise empty road. She didn't see who was in the buggy, but she waved.

"Even now?" asked Mark, drawing her attention to him.

"I'd like to say *ja*, but he's changing."

"No teenager wants to confess his troubles to an

adult." He wore a grim expression. "Every teen thinks what they're enduring is something no one else in the history of the world has had to deal with it. On days like today, when he's having fun, he can turn morose faster than you can snap your fingers."

"You want to help Daryn, ain't so?"

"Of course. He's my youngest brother. I want to spare him from making as many mistakes as I can."

"I know you do, but making mistakes is one of the ways we learn."

"Not for me."

Her eyes widened. "You never made mistakes?"

"Not like the one I fear he may have made."

"I don't understand."

He motioned with his head for her to follow as he walked along the road. She did, curious what he had to say that he didn't want anyone to overhear.

When he paused about halfway between Hosea's farmhouse and its neighbor, he pulled several articles out of his coat pocket. She took them when he handed them to her. Three black gloves. Plain, everyday gloves.

She looked at him and saw his face was blank. That meant, she'd come to learn, he was trying to hide his most powerful emotions. About plain, everyday gloves?

"So?" she asked, not sure what else to say.

"I found these on the beach."

"I don't understand."

He took the top one and turned it over. "See the red paint?"

"*Ja.* Two of these gloves have red paint on them. Not a lot, so I'm not sure why someone threw them away. Could they be lost gloves?"

His voice became darker. "I don't think so. Listen…"

Kirsten did while Mark told her about the graffiti on

their neighbor's boat. She interrupted to ask, "Why do you think Daryn painted those words?"

"I didn't say that."

"You didn't have to." She arched her brows. "How could you tell if one is Daryn's glove? Lots of men wear gloves like this."

"I know."

"You could ask him."

"I could, but I can't remember the last time he gave me a straight answer to a question."

"He did when you asked him how the game was going." She handed him the gloves.

Putting them into his pocket, he said, "*Ja*, that's true."

"Why do you assume the worst with him?"

"For the same reason you seem to assume the best about Theo. Experience."

Kirsten blinked back abrupt and unexpected tears at Mark's discouraged answer. She prayed for the words to reassure him. How could she urge Mark to risk making a mistake and baring his wounded soul when she was so leery of doing the same?

That question bounced through her head the rest of the afternoon after Mark had gone to join the other men while Kirsten found herself at loose ends. She wanted to go home, but must wait until the rest of the family decided to leave. She was glad to see Theo had joined the other kids playing volleyball. Janelle and *Aenti* Helga were enjoying talking with other women, especially when the topic turned to how *Aenti* Helga's root beer was on many tables in the community since she'd placed most of her supply at the farm shop.

"You look as if you could use a friend," said a sweet voice from behind her.

"Aveline!" She smiled at her friend who lived in another district along the bay.

Aveline Lampel was barely five feet tall, and her friend looked even shorter when she stood beside Kirsten. Her glistening red hair was visible beneath her bonnet, but her bright green eyes gleamed. Freckles, scattered across her cheeks, made her look no older than Theo. In truth, she was a year older than Kirsten's age of twenty-four.

With a laugh, Aveline replied, "My *mamm* decided to stop by your house to chat with your *aenti*. When you weren't home, she decided she'd come to see Helga here. You know how useless it is to try to change *Mamm*'s mind."

Kirsten smiled. Agreeing didn't seem right, but she'd seen for herself how inflexible Chalonna Lampel was. Grateful Aveline hadn't inherited her *mamm*'s temperament, she said, "It doesn't matter why you're here. I'm glad you are."

"Me, too." Her voice dropped to a whisper. "I saw you walking along the road with Mark Yutzy. So you're getting quite chummy with him, ain't so?"

Kirsten wagged her finger at her friend. "Don't look for something that's not there. We aren't walking out together. Mark simply asked me for advice on how to help his brother, and I've been sharing what I've learned from living with Theo."

"It's better he asked you for advice than me. Maybe Daryn is adventurous like my brothers. They were always looking for ways to have adventures. That's what they called them. Adventures. Even when it was borrowing a neighbor's car and taking it for a joyride into a tree or losing several acres of corn because they started a campfire to cook hot dogs too close to the field." Her bright green eyes twinkled. "Of course, I wanted to join them on their adventures."

"You did?"

"Why so surprised? Didn't you and your friends get into trouble like that?"

"Not my friends. Believe it or not, *I* was the one who was adventurous."

"I don't believe it. I don't know anyone who's as wary as you are."

"Now."

"So what happened to change you so much?"

As she had before, Kirsten considered opening up to her friend and telling Aveline about the missteps her heart had led her into making. *How can I put the past behind me if I let it get dredged up over and over?* Instead of the truth, she replied with the answer she'd devised on her way to Prince Edward Island. "I grew up, I guess."

She realized her friend wasn't listening to her when Aveline looked around her and smiled. Looking over her shoulder, Kirsten saw Mark walking toward them. She was about to introduce him to her friend, but Aveline beat her to it.

"I'm Aveline Lampel." She smiled up at him. "You're Mark Yutzy. I've seen you around Shushan. Remember? I was the silly person at the hardware store asking you if you could help me find the right sized nails for my *daed.*"

He grinned. "How's the work going on his well house?"

"Great! You should stop by and see it. *Daed* would like to meet the person who helped me pick out the exact nails he wanted."

When they laughed, Kirsten did her best to join in.

She clasped her hands in front of her and made sure there was an innocuous expression on her face. That wasn't easy when she felt as if a tornado and an earthquake were occurring at the same time in her center. Slowing her breathing to try to steady the storm, she didn't want to examine why she was suffused with envy at how easily her friend chatted with Mark.

No, she wasn't going to let her thoughts go in that direction. The only reason she might have for being jealous would have been if she and Mark were walking out together and he flirted with another woman.

And that wasn't going to happen. Aveline was right. Kirsten was extremely wary, and she had *gut* reasons to be. Most especially her promise to herself that she was done walking out with men whose priorities in life didn't include her.

Chapter Six

Sunlight shone through the windows on Monday afternoon and glittered on the furniture. Kirsten looked around the room in satisfaction. She'd been hired by a real estate agent to prepare the house for viewings. The owners had already gone to their winter home in Florida a month ago, leaving the house to be sold furnished.

It had plenty of windows. Each one had a wreath hanging from a red velvet ribbon. Pale walls were the same soft blue-gray as the bay on a cloudy day. A huge fireplace separated the living room from the dining room and kitchen, and it was easy to imagine a fire leaping on the large hearth, sending waves of heat to the far corners of the expansive rooms. Over her head, a loft was edged by a wrought iron and glass railing decorated with greens and lights. Two bedrooms and a bath were upstairs while two more bedrooms and two additional bathrooms were in the annex beyond the state-of-the-art kitchen with its white and rustic red cabinets.

She savored the opportunity to work in a house like this one where the light was brilliant and the view of the bay stretched as far as she could see. She seemed cut off from everything and everyone except God's beautiful creation. She could let her thoughts wander. No thinking about her mortifying past. No wondering about checking up on Janelle's work again the day after tomorrow at the Yutzys' or whether she'd have to caution *Aenti* Helga—again!—not to speak of what she'd seen in clients' homes. No worries that she was already too attracted to Mark Yutzy.

At the thought of Mark, who refused to be pushed out of her mind, Kirsten reached for the dust mop. She'd give the maple floors a final polish and make sure her footprints were wiped away. No sense in lingering. Her sense of tranquility had vanished like a popped soap bubble. She'd already taken the rest of her supplies out to her buggy. She walked backward, glancing over her shoulder to make sure she didn't bump into a table holding a lamp or a piece of abstract glass sculpture.

The quiet was broken by a frantic knock on the front door. The noise startled Kirsten. She leaned her mop against the sofa and wove her way around the tables and chairs into the front hall.

"Coming!" she called as the knocking continued, harder and more frenzied.

She reached for the antique-looking latch on the door. A spark of static electricity snapped her fingers, and she jerked back with a yelp. Before she could reach out again, the door swung open, letting in the icy air.

"Are you okay?" asked Mark.

She composed herself enough to answer instead of demanding he explain why he was pounding on the door. How had he known where she was? Or maybe he wasn't looking for her. That made no sense. Why else would he be at an unoccupied house?

"Ja," she said as soon as she regained her voice. She tapped the latch, then wiggled her finger. "I got zapped

by static electricity. A risk when I'm running a dust map over a floor on a cold, clear day."

"Did you burn yourself?" He took her hand in his much wider one, cupping it as if it were a tiny bird.

Her answer stuck in her throat as she savored the light caress of his skin on hers.

"It doesn't look burned," he said.

"It isn't." Surprised by how difficult it was to lift her hand away from his, she asked, "What's going on?"

When Mark gave his head a shake, setting his almost white hair fluttering under his straw hat, she wondered if he had been as lost in the delight of their hands touching as she'd been.

Don't be silly, she warned herself. He was, without question, a logical man, focused on making his farm and his brother successes.

"I've been looking for you," Mark said. "I was about to give up when I saw your buggy out front."

"Looking for me? Why?"

"I need your help."

"My help? With what?" Her face grew cold. Not from the wind, but from deep within her. "Has something happened with Daryn?"

"No." He rubbed his brow. "Or at least I hope he didn't have anything to do with it."

"To do with *what*?"

"The explosion at the Celtic Knoll Farm Shop."

She stared at him in disbelief. An explosion? At the shop run by his cousin?

"Is everyone okay?" she managed to ask.

"*Ja*. Nobody was there when the explosion happened. Mattie discovered it when she opened the store this morning."

"Are they sure it was an explosion?"

He nodded. "It sprayed debris everywhere. If some-one had been in the shop when it happened, they could have been hurt or worse."

"What exploded?"

Her *aenti* Helga's root beer? She prayed not, but it was possible. Two years ago, before they had left Ontario, every bottle her *aenti* had made had blown off its cap in the cellar, coating the shelves, the walls, the floor joists overhead with sticky brown syrup. It had taken a week to clean off every can of vegetables and meat and fruit as well as the shelves and floors. A month later, they still had found sticky spots. It'd been important to clean to prevent bugs from having a feast.

At the store with its higher roof, the eruption could have gone much farther, splattering the curve of the Quonset hut walls. Had it broken windows? She wanted to groan. Replacing them might take every penny she'd set aside over the summer to get them through the win-ter until her company was better established.

There was also the matter of the money *Aenti* Helga had planned to make from the sales of her root beer. Without those funds, there might not be enough cash to get through the next month.

"Finding what exploded," Mark said in a discour-aged tone, "took a while."

"*Aenti* Helga—"

He caught her hands in his again, shocking her into silence. Folding one hand over the other, he pancaked them between his palms. "It wasn't Helga's root beer. I checked that shelf first. The bottles were intact, except for a couple that fell and broke."

"Then what caused the explosion?"

"Cans of tomato sauce."

Relief surged through her, but it wasn't as strong as

the warm ripples radiating out from their hands. His skin was toughened by hard work. There was a gentleness in his touch that touched the raw edges of her heart.

"Oh, that's going to be a real mess," she said, then wished she'd remained silent when he released her hands and stuck his into the pockets of his coat.

"You've got that right. Can you come over and look it over? We don't know where to begin with the cleanup."

"Let me get packed up. Then I'll drive right over there."

"I'll help."

She directed him to the kitchen where she'd left her broom and other supplies. With his help, she was able to get everything to the buggy in a single trip. She locked the door behind her and dropped the ring that held her clients' keys into her purse.

"I hope they'll understand why I had to pull you away," Mark said as he lowered the buggy flap.

"I was just finishing up." She motioned toward his buggy. "Go ahead. I'll follow you."

"*Danki*, Kirsten."

"I'm glad I can help, but I'm sorry this has happened."

"Me, too." He didn't say anything else.

However, she saw the anxious lines gouged into his face. She wondered how tightly his plans for his future on the Island were tied up with his cousin's.

Mark took a deep breath before he walked into the shop's Quonset hut. At least three windows were cracked. He hadn't noticed that before when he'd come to help Mattie figure out what had happened. They'd have to be replaced as soon as possible. The winter cold could seep in and ruin the vegetables. Dents in the curved metal would have to be hammered out and repainted. The lower ones he and his cousins could handle, but they'd have to call in someone with a scissor lift to get high enough to reach the damage on the top of the roof.

He was less sure how they'd remove the tomato stains from the concrete floor. It'd been painted and sealed, so that might save it. Vegetables and fruit had been splattered with red sauce, so those couldn't be sold. Mattie couldn't risk someone with allergies buying and eating the produce. Perhaps she could find a place to donate the food in the bins. It was a shame to throw away so much fresh food.

It had been a relief to discover the baked goods had been spared. They were displayed in the opposite direction from the explosion. He was glad, too, that the *kaffi* machine hadn't been hit. Once he showed Kirsten around the building so she could evaluate the damage, he would have a nice hot cup.

Mattie and Daisy came forward to meet them. The exuberant Daisy said, "Look at the mess. Boppi Lynn is glad she didn't get red on her."

He grinned at his cousins. Bending, he squeezed the doll's cloth hand. "I'm glad, too, Boppi Lynn." He knew when Daisy spoke about her doll's "feelings," she usually was talking about her own.

"*Danki* for coming, Kirsten," Mattie said, motioning for them to follow her. "I'll show you where the blast occurred."

"Blast?" Kirsten asked.

Mattie smiled. "That's what Daisy is calling it, and it seems somehow friendlier than explosion. Ain't so?"

"I don't like either," Mark grumbled.

His cousin waved aside his words. "It's not about liking or not liking. It's about handling the challenges that get in our way, and counting our blessings that nothing worse happened."

Chastised by his cousin's deep faith, Mark was silent as he walked with the others around the end of the first row of shelves. Was that what he was supposed to be doing with his brother? Handling the challenges and counting his blessings that the situation wasn't worse?

What if it was worse than he knew? He touched his coat pocket where the black knit gloves hid. He'd planned on talking to Daryn about them last night, but his brother had gone out to a youth event with friends. At least, that was where Daryn had said he was going.

Mark clenched his hands by his sides. He loathed not being able to trust his brother. It hadn't been this way when they lived in Ontario, but Mark hadn't been responsible for him then. As he had before, he had to wonder what their parents had been thinking when they sent Daryn to Prince Edward Island.

Thoughts of his brother vanished when he rounded the end of the shelves. Red sauce ran past other cans and bottles and dripped onto the floor.

"How many burst?" he asked as Kirsten walked past him, her gaze focused on the disaster.

"Two whole cases," Mattie replied. "Twenty-four large cans in each case."

That explained why so much red was splashed everywhere. Again his fingers wandered toward the pocket holding the gloves he'd found. He was amazed at how much relief he felt. Because he'd been wondering if some of the red was paint? There had been trouble in the farm shop before it opened, but nothing in the months since the local constable spoke with the miscreants who'd tried to force Mattie and Daisy out of the building.

If it hadn't been vandalism, then how had the cans exploded?

Were others on the edge of detonating, too?

None of the cans had been near the stove that heated the shop, so they couldn't have fallen on an open flame and heated until the pressure built up in the can enough to send the cans flying across the shop.

Walking to where Kirsten was examining a shelf, one hand over her nose and mouth, he asked, "What do you think happened?"

"I had no idea it was this bad." She stood straighter and faced him. "From what you said, I thought it was a few cans. Not this many."

"I didn't mean to play down the mess." Pieces of tomato clung to the metal spines arching overhead. Two windows were plastered in red, and one had an aluminum can stuck in it. "You can see why we need your help."

"You're going to need a lot more help than I can give."

"The community will step up to help as they did before the shop opened."

"More help than that." Her voice was bleak. "We should be grateful nobody was in the store."

"How long," Mattie asked as she joined them, "do you think it'll take before we can reopen?"

"I'm not sure." Kirsten turned, taking in the devastation. "There are a lot of things to be considered."

"Like what?"

Before Kirsten could answer, Mark said, "Let's talk about it over some *kaffi*."

Mattie nodded and turned toward the machine that wasn't far from the cash register.

Kirsten grabbed Mattie's arm to halt her. "You can't eat or drink anything in here."

"What?" he asked, astonished. "This is a food store, Kirsten. Are you saying something is wrong with *everything*?"

When Mattie blanched, he understood. Mattie had sunk every penny she had into the shop as well as money from her family. Throwing it all out would be catastrophic.

"I don't know yet." Kirsten looked at Mattie and Daisy who'd come closer to her sister and was clutching Mattie's hand. "How old were those cans?"

"Not that old," Mattie replied. "I check the BB/MA dates on cans before I put them on the shelves."

"What is BB/MA?" Mark asked.

"BB is 'best by,' the date that the food in the cans is at its best to use. MA is the same thing in French. *Meilleur avant.* The food remains *gut* for a month or two longer." Her brows lowered as she frowned. "None of those cans of tomatoes were old. I received them a few days ago, and Daisy and I put them on the shelves yesterday." Her forehead threaded. "I don't understand how this happened."

Kirsten abruptly clapped her hands. "Get out! Right now!"

"What?" asked Mark.

She motioned as if trying to sweep them out the door. "Go!" Her voice hardened. "I'll explain once we're outside."

"Why should—?"

She didn't let him finish. "Go! As fast as you can." She grabbed the wheelchair and pushed it so hard Daisy rocked against the seat.

Boppi Lynn tumbled out. Mark caught the doll, seized Mattie by the arm and steered her past the door. He started to hand the doll to Daisy, but Kirsten halted him.

"Did it fall on the floor?" she asked.

Daisy shook her head. "Mark saved her."

Kirsten gestured for Mark to hand the doll to Daisy. "Keep Boppi Lynn close to you, Daisy. We don't want her getting sick."

"Sick?" Daisy's eyes grew wide.

Mark reached behind him to close the door, but Kirsten halted him.

"No!" she exclaimed. "Don't shut the door! The more air circulating the better."

"What do you suspect?" he asked.

She gave him a steady look. "Something made those cans explode. Until we know what caused it, we've got to assume it was botulism. We can't breathe the spores in. It's too dangerous."

Mark grabbed Daisy's wheelchair again and rolled it toward the buggies in the parking lot. Mattie hurried alongside him. He glanced over his shoulder to see Kirsten walking toward the shop's door.

"What are you doing?" he called.

"I'll be right there."

She didn't go in, but walked beside the Quonset hut in steady steps from front to back. He heard her as she counted, "One. Two more. The same number on the other side."

Helping his cousins into their buggy, he folded Daisy's chair. Kirsten was walking toward them by the time he'd finished storing it in the back.

She glanced at the building. "If it's okay with you, I'll contact a disaster restoration company. There may be one in Shushan. If not, I'm sure there is in Charlottetown. They can rid the space of botulism spores as well as cleaning the high spots we can't reach. When they're done, we can clean up the rest."

"*Danki*, Kirsten," Mattie said with a wobbly smile.

"If you have trouble swallowing or blurred vision, go to your *doktor*. Do the same if you start to throw up." She looked from his cousins to him. "Don't ignore the symptoms. Getting medical help is vital."

"We will." Mattie picked up the reins and steered the buggy toward the road.

Mark released the breath he'd been holding for longer than he'd guessed. It burst out of him in a sigh.

"This upsets you, ain't so?" Kirsten asked.

"I hate seeing Mattie so distressed."

Her laugh startled him. "Mattie? She's handling this well. You're the one who's as jumpy as a frog on a hot sidewalk."

"What? Who puts a frog on a hot sidewalk?"

"It's something my *grossmammi* used to say." She folded her arms. "Don't try to change the subject."

"I wasn't."

"Really?"

"No. That saying is strange. I've never heard it before."

"It's quite common where I—" She frowned. "You're doing it again. Changing the subject. Let's start over. This upsets you, ain't so?"

He opened his mouth to reply, then closed it when her eyes narrowed to dark brown slits. "You're right. It does. Having those cans burst is so unlikely that I can't help thinking there must be a cause other than botulism."

"Don't look for trouble."

"Don't *you* think it's odd those cans blew up at the same time?"

She shrugged. "I don't know. That's why I'm going to contact someone who can get Mattie answers. I realize this is tough for everyone, especially you."

"Why especially me?"

"Because you like order."

"I do."

"You don't have to sound defensive about it."

He took a breath before answering. "I didn't realize I had. I didn't intend to." He swept out an arm toward the Quonset hut. "I know how hard my cousins have worked to get this place open. To have something like this happen—something that makes no sense—seems unfair."

"Nobody ever said life was going to be fair."

"Platitudes don't help."

Her brows rose, but she nodded. "You're right. The best thing to do is get the cleanup underway. Let me—"

When she looked past him, Mark turned to see a familiar buggy coming toward them. Why was Mattie coming back to the shop?

He got his answer when his cousin stopped, opened the door on her side of the buggy and said, "I almost forgot, Kirsten. Will you let Janelle know she shouldn't come in tomorrow?"

"Come in?" Kirsten repeated.

"For work. She was supposed to start working here tomorrow."

"Oh… Okay, I'll tell her."

Mark watched Kirsten as the buggy drove away a second time. He'd never seen Kirsten so ramrod straight. She acted as if moving a single muscle would shatter her.

She was shocked her cousin had taken another job and hadn't mentioned it to her. He could almost hear the thoughts caroming through her head. Or at least the thoughts that would have been in his.

Why hadn't Janelle told her?

How was Kirsten going to handle Janelle's clients too?

Was her business going to survive such a setback?

His fingers ached to curve around her shoulders

and offer her comfort as she faced a situation as dire as Mattie's and Daisy's. The ache spread up his arms that longed to draw her within them and hold her until her troubles faded away. He imagined her softening against him.

Swallowing hard, Mark knew he was being a *dummkopf.* She had enough troubles with her family, and he'd already stacked more on her with Daryn and the shop.

"You didn't know Janelle was planning to work at the farm shop, ain't so?" he asked.

"No." She didn't face him.

Without another word, she walked to her buggy and climbed in. She didn't look in his direction when she drove away. He had no idea what he would have said to her when her cousin's decision might well ring a death knell for Kirsten's business.

Chapter Seven

Kirsten didn't mention Janelle's new job when she returned home for supper. Speaking in anger wouldn't help them. She wanted to avoid upsetting her *aenti* and Theo.

As she walked into the kitchen, she wondered where Theo was. It wasn't like her cousin to be late for a meal.

"He's out with his friends," *Aenti* Helga replied to Kirsten's query while she continued to slice bread with smooth strokes.

"His *Englisch* friends?"

Putting aside the knife, she picked up the platter piled high with the bread. "I'm sure we'll meet them soon. There aren't that many families along the bay."

Janelle walked in, started to speak and then paused when her gaze linked with Kirsten's. An embarrassed flush rose up her cheeks, and she looked as if she'd rather be anywhere else other than in the kitchen with Kirsten.

As she'd acted for the past few days, Kirsten realized. Her cousin had been avoiding her.

"Janelle, can I speak with you?" Kirsten asked, not wanting to put off delivering the message from Mattie.

"Can't right now. Got to—" She ran out of the kitchen and up the stairs.

Aenti Helga shook her head. "I don't know how one slight girl can sound like a herd of elephants."

Kirsten let her *aenti* change the subject to the house she'd cleaned that day and how many different and interesting things the clients owned. Though the words washed over her, hardly noticed, Kirsten was aware of glances *Aenti* Helga kept aiming in her direction. The older woman knew Kirsten didn't like her talking about their clients' homes.

Kirsten was as determined not to get into an argument with her *aenti* as she was with her cousin. She helped carry food into the dining room, nodded to Theo when he blew into the house with the icy wind and sat at the table to share silent grace with the family.

For the first time in months, she wondered what *Mamm* and *Daed* were doing. They ate supper earlier than *Aenti* Helga did. She could imagine *Daed* leaning back in his chair and patting his stomach and telling *Mamm* she'd prepared another *wunderbaar* meal. A craving to see them sliced into her. Homesickness? For her family, *ja*, but not for the community she couldn't face. To hear the whispers and see the stares following her... No, she didn't want to go through that again.

She had to deal with the situation in her family in Prince Edward Island. She couldn't put it off. Janelle hadn't said a word to her through the meal and kept glancing at her *mamm*. Was she looking for an excuse to leave the table?

Kirsten couldn't let that happen before she passed along the message as she'd promised. "Janelle, Mattie asked me to tell you that you shouldn't come to work tomorrow."

"She did?" asked Janelle, blushing.

At the same time, her *mamm* frowned. "Why would Mattie care about Janelle's work tomorrow?"

The girl lowered her head. "Because I took a job at the farm shop."

"That's not a *gut* idea," *Aenti* Helga said, setting her sandwich on her plate.

"I want a job."

"You've got a job. You work for Ocean Breezes."

"I quit."

When?, Kirsten wanted to ask but didn't get a chance before *Aenti* Helga asked in a taut tone, "So you're not working for us any longer?"

Kirsten bit her lip before she reminded her *aenti* the business was Kirsten's, not *Aenti* Helga's. One problem at a time...

Janelle stood. "I don't like cleaning houses. Mattie is going to teach me to use the cash register as well as how to stock the shelves." She put her hands on the table on either side of her plate. "Please understand, Kirsten. I want to do something with people. When I'm cleaning house, I don't often see anyone else. They're gone before I get there, and they don't return until I'm done."

"Sit down," her *mamm* said. "You can't quit without giving us fair warning." She held up her hand. "This isn't up for debate, Janelle. If you want to work at the shop, that's fine, but you have to continue with your house-cleaning jobs until Kirsten can find someone to take your place."

"I'll be working every second of the day," wailed the teen.

"Until I find someone," Kirsten said, having sympathy for her cousin. She glanced at Theo who seemed unaware of the conversation or wisely was staying out of it.

Janelle became calm. "What if I know someone who might be interested?"

"That would be *wunderbaar*," Kirsten said, hoping whomever Janelle recommended would be more enthusiastic about doing a *gut* job than her cousin was.

"Let me talk to my friend tomorrow, and, if she's interested, then I'll let you know so you can hire her." She picked up the bowl of applesauce and spooned half of it on her plate as if she'd rediscovered her appetite. "I should be able to continue to do a house or two. Mattie said she couldn't give me a lot of hours during the winter, because the store isn't busy then."

"Danki." Kirsten smiled. She hadn't expected Janelle to be so reasonable after her cousin had slunk out of the kitchen.

"I can do the Yutzys because they're close by."

Kirsten was startled. "Why that house? You know how particular Mark is about his house. I thought you'd be happy not to have to go back."

She raised her eyes toward the ceiling and shook her head. "You told him I would do a better job, and I want him to see that I can. Not just one time, but over and over."

"I appreciate that, Janelle." She did and couldn't help wondering if her cousin might be growing up…at least a little. She wasn't so sure when Janelle went on.

"Not that I can do much *gut* there. The Yutzys' old house is about to fall apart. The slightest puff of a breeze makes it groan. None of the windows can be opened because Mark jammed wood into them so they won't fall down. For a guy who was a woodworker, he's let his house go to ruin."

"He's been busy with his crops."

"That's no excuse for letting the house go to seed."

She smiled at what she seemed to think was a jest. "Crops. Seed. Get it?"

"That's pretty lame," Theo said as he reached for another slice of bread.

"You're sorry you didn't think of it first."

Aenti Helga forestalled a possible argument by changing the subject to the cookie exchange she hoped to host. "You'll help, ain't so, Kirsten?"

"You can count on me." She enjoyed making cookies as much as her cousins enjoyed eating them. Baking a few extra batches would allow her to try different recipes. She'd find time, even if she had to take over Janelle's clients temporarily. "Let me know when you want them."

"I'm hoping to have it the week before Christmas. Quite a few members of the community are planning to head back to Ontario to see family for the holidays, so it would be nice to give them something to take with them on the journey."

"Which means I should avoid making frosted cookies."

"You can make them for me," Theo piped up.

The tension sifted away, and Kirsten began to see that not having her whole family working for her might not be a bad thing. They'd brought their work home with them too often, and it had begun to taint their relationships.

God, danki *for knowing what is best for us when we can't see it for ourselves.*

Over the next few days, Mark grew more impressed with Kirsten's knowledge of how to clean the farm shop and make it safe again. She'd been right. Tests had confirmed there had been something wrong with the cans' contents. The Canadian Food Inspection Agency had been contacted, and a recall went out to prevent other stores from suffering what the Celtic Knoll Farm Shop had.

Fans were brought in by the mediation company from Shushan to blow botulism spores out before customers were allowed inside. Kirsten's precautions hadn't ended there. She'd insisted everyone cleaning the walls, shelves and floors wear a respirator mask. Yesterday, after three days of steady ventilation and the replacement of the broken windows, she'd changed her requirements to a simple paper mask.

He tugged at his. He'd like to be rid of it, but he'd wait until the all clear was given. Getting ill would delay his plans for returning to work on his house. Old-timers on the Island warned the first snowfall could be any day, and he needed to get up and check the roof that seemed to be sagging at one side.

But two *gut* things had happened this week. Janelle had come back to the house yesterday and done a superb job of cleaning what she could. The kitchen was torn apart as were some of the walls, but the bathroom sparkled, and the floors had been wiped clean of plaster dust.

Even more important, the strain had begun to lessen—slightly—between him and Daryn. The day after the explosion in the farm shop, Mark had decided he'd give Kirsten's suggestion a try. He'd asked Daryn to help take out the kitchen cabinets and the wiring left by the house's previous, *Englisch* owner. His brother had responded with enthusiasm.

"I like breaking things and tearing them apart," Daryn had said with a big grin. "There's a sledgehammer in the barn."

"Let's start with a crowbar and a hammer. Breaking through walls without knowing what's there is stupid."

"But lots of fun."

Glad to see his little brother's smile, Mark chuckled. "I agree. I'm planning to take down a couple of those wobbly outbuildings next spring. Those will make good sledgehammer fodder."

Daryn's grin faded. "You'll have sent me home by then."

"I'm sure I can persuade *Daed* and *Mamm* to let you stay a little while longer. It'd be *gut* to have someone else around when I demolish those buildings."

"They won't agree."

"How do you know?"

"Because they don't want me to have fun, and they don't think I can do anything right." He slammed his hands into his pockets. "Just like you do."

"I think you do things right. I wouldn't have asked for your help otherwise."

"You don't think I mess up all the time?"

"Not all the time," Mark drawled.

Daryn started to fire a retort, then paused and grinned. "But I want to have some fun."

"Work can be fun."

"For you maybe. I don't want to be a potato farmer."

"What do you want to do?"

He'd been surprised when Daryn had said, "I've been thinking about raising beef cattle."

"Why did you choose that?"

"I read an article about Amish ranches out west where they raise beefers, and it sounds like a great life. Riding and roping and tending to a herd." His nose had wrinkled. "Better than potatoes."

"You're right. Potatoes don't run away and have to be rounded up by lasso."

When his brother had laughed instead of firing back

a snarky comment, Mark had been amazed. Kirsten's advice to treat Daryn like an equal and not like a *kind* seemed to work.

Kirsten was handling everything for the farm shop's cleanup with the same efficiency and insight. She directed the *Englisch* crew with an ease Mark had to envy.

That was why he was surprised to discover Kirsten in the shop wearing a dismayed expression. She'd confronted every crisis-in-the-making until now with a positive attitude.

"What's wrong? Are you still upset with Janelle for getting a job here?" he asked.

"No. We've talked that over, and I'm going to find a replacement for Janelle. Even after I can hire and train someone else, Janelle has offered to continue doing a couple of houses through the winter. Like yours, for example."

"Why my house?" He watched as a pair of hefty *Englischers* carried one of the large fans into the farm shop. He couldn't wait for the sound level to be normal. Working in the Quonset hut had been as noisy and windy as he imagined standing behind a jet plane engine would have been. "If you'd asked me, I would have said mine would be the first one she'd want to get rid of. She did do a *gut* job yesterday. I thought you'd want to know."

"*Danki.* I'm glad you feel you got your money's worth." Her eyes twinkled.

It took him a moment, then he realized what she meant. "Janelle didn't clean as if the job was a freebie. She worked hard, especially when it came to getting dust out of the house. But I'm still surprised that she wants to keep working at my house."

"I was amazed myself, but she wants to make it right." She clasped her hands in front of her. "Janelle has a friend who might be interested in the job. I hope she'll be a *gut* fit. Until I can hire someone else, Janelle is going to have to balance two jobs."

"The shop looks great."

Kirsten looked around, and her eyes crinkled with a smile. "The mediation company has done an excellent job."

He nodded, not wanting to embarrass her by saying *she* had made what seemed impossible possible. The shop was clean and the shelves restocked. The fresh fruit and vegetable bins were empty, but Mattie had been assured by her supplier there would be a delivery early next week. The day after that, the doors to the Celtic Knoll Farm Shop would reopen.

"I brought potatoes," he said.

"*Gut.* You're right on time. I was about to leave. I was waiting for them to remove these fans." She held out a ring of keys. "I'll leave these with you."

"Where are Mattie and Daisy? I thought they'd be here."

"They had to run home to get supper ready for you and your cousins. Mattie said she usually prepares something the night before, but last night, she was so exhausted she fell into bed before taking her shoes off."

"She does too much for us."

"If you ask her, she'd say you do too much for her."

A faint smile curved along his lips, tilting his mask to an odd angle. "You're right." Without a pause, he asked, "How about that cup of *kaffi* we never got before you chased us out of the shop? A new café has opened near the Sea Gull Holiday Cottages."

"I thought that the building wasn't opening for another month."

"The lights are on, and the owners have hung a big

banner out front announcing they're in business. Looks like it might be a soft opening so they can work out the kinks before they have their official grand opening. What do you say? By the time I'm done unpacking the potatoes, I'm going to be thirsty, and *kaffi* sounds great."

"I don't think—"

"Don't think, Kirsten. Say *ja*. You've been working hard, and the only way I can imagine convincing you to relax is to sit there with you."

"I don't know."

"Why not?"

It was a loaded question, and one that Kirsten didn't want to answer. How could she explain to Mark about how her skin crawled at the idea of going to a café? That was the kind of place where Loyal had met the woman he chose over Kirsten. The best *barista*. That's what he'd called the woman, never once mentioning her given name as he stumbled over his words while telling Kirsten he didn't want to continue their relationship. Mark wanted to take her to a place like that.

He isn't Loyal, she reminded herself. *Loyal hadn't been loyal.* A tinge of hysteria enveloped that thought, and she pushed it away. Five years had passed. Loyal had moved on long ago. It was time for her to do the same.

Trying to keep her voice light, she mused, "I wonder if they serve chai lattes."

"Chai lattes? What are those?"

"Chai is a tea mixture with cinnamon and ginger. Latte means it's combined with steam milk." She smiled. "It's like drinking a liquid oatmeal cookie."

"Let's go and see."

Knowing she'd be disappointed if she didn't agree, she nodded. She had to confront her past, but more enticing was the idea of spending time talking with Mark. Not about their work or their families, but about whatever they wanted. It was something they'd never done, and it sounded *wunderbaar*.

Kirsten took a deep breath of the fresh air as she looked toward the west where the sun was sinking quickly. Days were so much shorter now at the end of November. Mark brought the buggy to a stop near a hitching rail next to a large building that looked as if it'd been a dairy barn.

It was illusion. The building had been built over the past summer. No one had been quite sure what it was going to be. Rumors whispered it might house a glass-blowing shop and a pottery or a collection of *doktors*' offices. A few tongues had wagged about a new restaurant or a yoga studio, something aimed more at locals than tourists because it'd been started so late in the season, too late to capture the final visitors of the year.

Instead a sign had been hung out front announcing the coming of Shushan Bay Beans. A cartoonish figure of a dark brown *kaffi* bean was emblazoned on the white sign with bright red letters. The sign was set by the road. A smaller version of the sign hung by the front door on the left side of the broad front porch. He guessed tables and chairs would be set out there once the weather turned warm, but nobody would want to sit and sip *kaffi* when the wintry wind blew in from the icy bay.

"Here we are," he said needlessly.

"I can't wait to find out what they serve." Kirsten slid open the door on her side of her buggy and stepped out. She tightened her scarf around her neck and pulled it up over her nose as she walked toward the porch steps.

He paused long enough to tie the horse to the hitching post, then hurried to where Kirsten stood by the door. Opening it, he motioned for her to precede him into the café.

Two people were working behind the long counter. Wood floors gleamed underfoot. The menu was written in chalk on a long, tall blackboard set behind the counter where registers that looked like handheld computers waited for customers. Black metal plates held together the unpainted beams that crisscrossed the ceiling. A fireplace divided the space into two, with sliding doors on either side. He guessed they could be closed to allow for a private space on the far side of the fireplace.

Next to one side of the fireplace, a tall tree was covered with Christmas ornaments. They were white and gold to match the ribbon garland woven among its branches. Birds with real feathers for their tails sat on gilded nests. A star that appeared to be made out of straw and rhinestones perched on the top of the tree. Lights twinkled on the tree. Overhead hung lamps with bulbs sprouting in every direction. The lamps dangled between hanging plants and shone down on the glass case which contained a few baked goods.

Kirsten bent to look at them. She was astonished the scones and muffins came in flavors like blueberry-lemon or lavender-vanilla or pumpkin spice.

Mark decided on a chocolate chip muffin and a simple cup of *kaffi*. He smiled when Kirsten chose a pumpkin spice scone to go with her chai latte. A few minutes later, the *barista* had put together their drinks and handed them their treats on plates decorated with the image of the *kaffi* bean on the sign out front.

Kirsten wondered why she'd hesitated to come to the *kaffi* café. It wasn't the same one where Loyal had met his *barista*, and even if it had been, that had happened years ago. She couldn't live her life stuck in the past, being drawn back as if a rubber band was wrapped around her middle. It was time to cut that band into so many pieces it couldn't ensnare her again.

Pausing to sprinkle cinnamon on her chai latte, Kirsten went with Mark to a table near the fireplace. The fresh, damp scent of pine needles was the perfect accent to her drink.

"Do you want to try it?" She held up the cup, and he leaned forward to sample the aromas wafting from it.

"You're right. It smells like an oatmeal cookie without raisins." He glanced down at his black *kaffi*. "I should be a bit more adventurous."

"Like your brother?"

His brows drew together. "Daryn?"

"*Ja. Adventurous* is the word my friend Aveline used to describe Daryn. Before you met her after church, she was talking to me about how her brothers got into trouble when they were Daryn's age, and they called them adventures." She shared some of Aveline's brothers' wild escapades.

Mark laughed when Kirsten got to the tale about Aveline's brothers convincing the kids in their neighborhood that they had an elephant in their barn. They'd charged the other *kinder* a loonie to pet the elephant's leg. The ruse had come to an end when someone discovered the leg was well-worn tire rubber the boys had scavenged from along the side of the road. The money they'd tricked the other kids out of had been sent as a contribution to the Mennonite Disaster Service to help with rebuilding after a flood along the US border in western Canada.

Taking a sip of her chai after finishing that story,

Kirsten said, "You think these stories are funny, but you're exasperated with Daryn."

"The stories are funny when they're happening to someone else's brothers." He stirred his *kaffi*. "And when one of the stories doesn't include how they painted insults on someone's boat."

She became serious. "You still think Daryn was involved in that?"

"I don't know."

"Did you show him the gloves?"

He shook his head. "I was going to, but then with the mess at the shop, I haven't had the time. When I didn't hear about any other vandalism, I figured it could wait. Have you heard anything new?"

"No. Maybe it was a onetime thing aimed at a particular fisherman."

"I'd like to believe that, but I don't."

"Why?"

"Just a feeling I've got." He continued stirring his *kaffi*. "I worry my parents were wrong to send Daryn here. He's helping around the house, but he may be getting bored. That's a sure way for him to start looking for trouble again."

Breaking a piece off her scone, she considered her answer. When it came, it was so obvious, she wondered why neither of them had considered it before.

"How about if we give the kids an adventure so they don't get bored?" she asked.

"I hope you're not suggesting we take a neighbor's car and head out across the Island or to find ruined tires to build an 'elephant.'"

She laughed. "The thought never crossed my mind. I was thinking about a different type of adventure. Let's take Janelle, Theo and Daryn into town and visit a thrift shop or two. Janelle wants a new clock for her room, and Theo is anxious to find some sports equipment. They might find what they're looking for in a thrift store in Shushan. You and Daryn can join us. Who knows what you'll find?"

"I don't know. Well, I do know. Spending an afternoon pawing through racks of worn clothing is something I don't want to do."

"I understand you're busy." There must be a way to convince Mark that his brother was more than an obligation. They could become friends, creating a friendship that would last the rest of their lives.

She'd tried to do that with Janelle, which was why she'd agreed to talk to Janelle's friend about working for Ocean Breezes. Maybe working together toward a common goal—finding a replacement for Janelle—would bring them closer. She hoped so.

And Theo. So far their relationship seemed comfortable. Yet she'd seen cracks. With her and with his *mamm.* He was growing up, testing his bounds, unsure what he wanted to be or whom. She wanted to help him. She wanted to help them avoid the mistakes she'd made.

"I *am* busy," Mark said, bringing her attention to him. "The house needs so much work."

She took a sip of her tea, then lowered the cup to the table. "It'll be fun. You'll see. Who knows what you might find?" Her smile broadened. "It'll give the kids a chance to get away while we can keep an eye on them."

"There is that, and I can't be too busy to help my brother." He nodded. "Let's have an adventure in Shushan."

She smiled as she reached for her cup. She didn't take a sip because her heart was doing jumping jacks. Had she been foolish to arrange for this outing when every image running through her head was focused on her and Mark as they walked along the main street, hand in hand?

Ja, she'd been silly to ask him to come with her and the kids, but this time wouldn't be like the past. She'd learned her lessons, and she wouldn't let her heart over-rule her brain.

Again.

Chapter Eight

Kirsten wasn't sure who was more excited about the trip into Shushan on Saturday: Janelle or her. It was a definite toss-up, and Kirsten was pleased the excursion could be arranged for a day when they didn't have any houses to clean. Janelle hadn't started at the shop yet because her friend, Amber Gouyou, an *Englischer* whose parents' house Janelle had cleaned several times, wouldn't be speaking with Kirsten until after the weekend.

What surprised Kirsten was how little excitement Theo showed when she brought up the idea at supper.

"Saturday?" His voice turned into a whine as he went on, "I was going to hang out with the guys then."

"Daryn is coming with us, so you'll have him at least."

He opened his mouth to reply, then shoved a forkful of macaroni and cheese in it. What he mumbled around the food was something Kirsten would have asked him to repeat if he hadn't kept cleaning his plate as if afraid someone was going to snatch it away from him.

She recognized his ploy, but she didn't call him on it. Theo used to talk too much, filling every silence in the wake of his *daed*'s death. Too often now, it seemed she had to pry words out of him.

Aenti Helga reached for another roll as she said, "It sounds like a fun day for all of you. Will you look for something for me?"

"What?" asked Janelle, excitement sparkling from her eyes.

"I'd like a larger Dutch oven," her *aenti* replied. "With your brother's appetite, the one I have isn't sufficient." She looked down into the serving bowl. "I'd hoped this batch of macaroni and cheese would last two meals. I don't know if it'll be enough for one."

Theo chuckled, but Kirsten noticed he didn't look her way through the rest of the meal. As soon as it was over, he bounded out the door to meet his friends.

Kirsten said nothing when *Aenti* Helga looked out the window to watch her son disappear into the shadows settling along the bay. Worry dug furrows into her *aenti*'s brow.

"It's late for him to be out when he has school tomorrow, ain't so?" *Aenti* Helga murmured, more to herself than to Kirsten.

"Are you asking me?" she asked.

"No." Her *aenti* gave her a pat on the shoulder. "I should be grateful he has friends to spend time with rather than worrying he's letting his chores slide. He's a *kind*. He needs to enjoy his friendships."

"He's taken on a lot."

Aenti Helga nodded. "Stanley never should have made him agree to be the man of the house."

Kirsten was glad when her *aenti* turned away because *Aenti* Helga would have seen the shock on her face. Not once since her *onkel* had died had her *aenti* spoken a negative word about him. It was as if *Aenti* Helga had buried alongside her husband all memories of their spats.

In fact, her *onkel*'s name had seldom been spoken once the funeral was over. Kirsten had gone to visit *Onkel* Stanley's grave at least once a month, but she had no idea if the others had been there since the day of his funeral. Sadness swelled inside her. The family wasn't trying to erase their memories of him, and she wished they'd speak of him more often. The studied way they'd begun to avoid mentioning him was worse, in her opinion, than lamenting his death.

Was it possible that after almost a year had passed, the walls each member of the family had built around themselves were beginning to tumble down? What a blessing if that were so! Everyone had been so careful about saying the wrong word they hadn't said anything.

On Saturday morning, Kirsten prayed as she waited for her cousins to come downstairs that the healing of their hearts was truly underway. Her hopes were dashed when a scowling Theo came down the stairs with his knees and half of his right shin visible through his trousers.

Behind him, his sister complained, "Kirsten, look at him! Tell him he can't go into town like that."

The boy halted on the bottom step. "What's wrong with how I look?"

"Your trousers have big holes in them," Janelle muttered as she walked past him. "How can you pretend you don't see those holes? They're big enough to drive a buggy through."

He looked down as if he hadn't noticed, then shrugged. "They're not that bad."

"Kirsten, tell him he can't go into town looking like a ragamuffin."

Hanging her purse over the newel post because she suspected sorting this out would take some time, Kirsten

Dear Reader,

I am writing to announce the launch of a huge **FREE BOOKS GIVEAWAY**... and to let you know that YOU are entitled to choose up to FOUR fantastic books that WE pay for.

Try **Love Inspired® Romance Larger-Print** books and fall in love with inspirational romances that take you on an uplifting journey of faith, forgiveness and hope.

Try **Love Inspired® Suspense Larger-Print** books where courage and optimism unite in stories of faith and love in the face of danger.

Or TRY BOTH!

In return, we ask just one favor: Would you please participate in our brief Reader Survey? We'd love to hear from you.

This FREE BOOKS GIVEAWAY means that your introductory shipment is completely free, <u>even the shipping</u>! If you decide to continue, you can look forward to curated monthly shipments of brand-new books from your selected series, always at a discount off the cover price! <u>Plus you can cancel any time</u>. Who could pass up a deal like that?

Sincerely

Pam Powers

Pam Powers
For Harlequin Reader Service

Complete the survey below and return it today to receive up to 4 FREE BOOKS and FREE GIFTS guaranteed!

FREE BOOKS GIVEAWAY
Reader Survey

1	2	3
Do you prefer books which reflect Christian values?	Do you share your favorite books with friends?	Do you often choose to read instead of watching TV?
◯ YES ◯ NO	◯ YES ◯ NO	◯ YES ◯ NO

YES! Please send me my Free Rewards, consisting of **2 Free Books from each series I select** and **Free Mystery Gifts**. I understand that I am under no obligation to buy anything, no purchase necessary see terms and conditions for details.

❑ **Love Inspired® Romance Larger-Print** (122/322 IDL GRQV)
❑ **Love Inspired® Suspense Larger-Print** (107/307 IDL GRQV)
❑ **Try Both** (122/322 & 107/307 IDL GRQ7)

FIRST NAME   LAST NAME

ADDRESS

APT.#   CITY

STATE/PROV.   ZIP/POSTAL CODE

EMAIL ❑   Please check this box if you would like to receive newsletters and promotional emails from Harlequin Enterprises ULC and its affiliates. You can unsubscribe anytime.

LI/LIS-122-FBG22_LI/LIS-122-FBGVR

▲ If offer card is missing write to: Harlequin Reader Service, P.O. Box 1341, Buffalo, NY 14240-8531 or visit www.ReaderService.com ▼

BUSINESS REPLY MAIL
FIRST-CLASS MAIL   PERMIT NO. 717   BUFFALO, NY

POSTAGE WILL BE PAID BY ADDRESSEE

HARLEQUIN READER SERVICE

PO BOX 1341

BUFFALO NY 14240-8571

NO POSTAGE
NECESSARY
IF MAILED
IN THE
UNITED STATES

sighed. Janelle was right. Theo knew that, too, but he wasn't going to admit it.

"Theo, those trousers are fine around the house," she said, praying again. This time for her cousins to compromise and cooperate. "You should wear something nicer for our trip into town."

"Told ya," Janelle said.

"That's enough!" Kirsten aimed a frown at Janelle, then another at Theo. She wished *Aenti* Helga hadn't had an early job, but then she wondered if her *aenti* would be able to handle the quarrel. Since *Onkel* Stanley's death, her *aenti* had avoided anything that hinted at confrontation.

Kirsten had been doing the same, she realized. How many times had she held her tongue when she should have spoken up? Too many.

That had to change. *Onkel* Stanley wouldn't want them walking around like shadows of themselves. He'd loved having his home filled with laughter, but he hadn't been reluctant to raise his voice.

Straightening her shoulders, Kirsten said, "Go and change, Theo, or we'll be late meeting Mark and Daryn."

The boy wore his most stubborn expression. "I don't wa—I can't change."

Kirsten didn't miss how he corrected himself. She was curious why he wanted to go shopping in clothing that looked ready for the garbage. The answer burst into her head. She'd seen *Englisch* teens in torn jeans, and, if *Aenti* Helga was right, Theo's new friends weren't plain. He must want to dress as they did. Telling him that he could wear *Englisch* clothing while he was on *rumspringa* wouldn't help. It was more than three years until Theo could choose his running around gang and venture out in what she hoped would be a short period of testing the parameters of a plain life until he decided to embrace being Amish.

"Why not?" she asked as if she hadn't noticed what he'd almost said.

He leaned his hand on the newel post at the bottom of the stairs. "These pants are the only ones I have."

"You have three other pairs of trousers."

"Two are in the laundry. The other one is ruined."

"Ruined?" Kirsten asked at the same time Janelle said, "They can't be ruined more than those."

"They are. I'll show you." He stamped toward the back porch.

Janelle rolled her eyes before walking in the opposite direction to peer out the window overlooking the road.

Kirsten took a step to go after Theo, but halted when he stormed back into the room.

He carried a pair of denim trousers like the ones he was wearing, except for the rips. He held them as if they were a pair of thin boards. "I left them out in the barn. I knew you wouldn't want them in the house."

"Can I see them?"

He handed them to her.

Frowning, she gasped when she realized he hadn't been keeping the legs out straight with his arms. The trousers were as stiff as if she'd ironed them with every bit of starch in the world. An odd odor drifted from them. A chemical odor she couldn't name.

"What's wrong with them?" she asked.

"Tar."

She looked at him in amazement as Janelle turned around and asked, "How did you get tar on them?"

"I was helping one of my friends' *daed* replace the roof on one of their outbuildings."

"*Mamm* will be furious!" Janelle gasped. "How could

you be so thoughtless? She just lost *Daed*. How could you risk your life climbing around on a roof when you saw what *Daed*'s death did to her? You're really stupid sometimes."

Theo looked so shocked Kirsten wasn't sure how he'd answer. Tears welled into his eyes, but he blinked them away as he yelled, "I'm not stupid. You are. You don't know what's going on."

"Janelle, Theo," Kirsten said. "Shouting won't get us anywhere."

"Wouldn't you be angry if she called you stupid?" demanded Theo.

"I would." She faced Janelle. "That was uncalled-for."

"*I*'m not the one who ruined my clothes by doing something…" She gulped.

Kirsten guessed she'd been about to say "something stupid," but had halted herself before she could infuriate her brother again. Giving Janelle's arm a squeeze, she said, "Theo, did you get up on the roof?"

"No. I wasn't up there, though I wanted to be. I was helping from the ground, but the tar got on me anyhow. I couldn't wear them again, so I tossed them into the trash."

Kirsten ran her finger along the trousers. The tar was thick, but that might help her save the trousers. If she could scrape off the tar, the fabric underneath might be salvageable.

"I think I can clean them," she said.

He rolled his eyes as his sister had moments before. "It's impossible."

"We'll see. In the meantime, let me have the trousers you're wearing, and I'll fix them."

"But…" He halted himself and said, "Okay."

Kirsten's smile returned when Theo went into the

bathroom and closed the door. A few moments later, the door reopened, and the trousers were tossed out. The door shut again.

Picking up Theo's trousers, she examined them. How had he gotten so many holes in them and in such a regular pattern? It looked as if a ladder had been cut into the denim. If he'd done this on purpose—and it appeared he had—*Aenti* Helga was going to have to put aside her grief and have a talk with her son.

She went to the mudroom to get her sewing kit from the basket where other items waited to be mended and tossed the stiff trousers on the top of the washing machine. Those she'd deal with between jobs on Monday. Sitting in a chair in the living room, she found thread close to the color of the ripped trousers. She smiled when Janelle came to sit next to her and picked up the other leg.

Kirsten sewed the slits on the right leg closed while Janelle did the same with the left. Her cousin's stitches were quicker and finer than her own, but Janelle would be horrified at the suggestion she make use of her skills. Whenever anyone suggested a quilting frolic, Janelle found an excuse not to participate.

"Danki," Kirsten said when Janelle finished.

"He's not going to be happy with how these look," her cousin mused as Kirsten worked on the last slit near the hem. "Maybe he'll be more careful."

They laughed at the same time. The idea of Theo worrying about his clothes was ludicrous. His head was too full of playing ball and doing his chores and playing more ball.

Kirsten broke the thread as she heard a wagon pull into the yard. Janelle snatched the trousers out of her hand, ran to the bathroom and stuffed them past the door. Fingers grasped them, then shut the door as foot-steps sounded on the front porch.

"I'll get it!" Janelle exclaimed.

Putting away her sewing kit, Kirsten looked around for her bonnet. She didn't see it. Where could she have left it? In the kitchen or the laundry room? She scanned the kitchen and didn't see her black bonnet. She went into the laundry room. It wasn't there either. Maybe in the mudroom.

Opening the door to the narrow space where they kept boots and extra mittens and gloves, she smiled when she saw her bonnet on top of the mending. She bent to pick it up, and her eyes were caught by a pair of sneakers shoved into the corner.

She didn't recognize them. Were they Theo's? If so, she'd never seen him wear the garish black-and-orange-and-yellow sneakers before. Red sand was caked on them from bottom to top. She grimaced and didn't touch them. When they returned home from Shushan, she'd have Theo slap the soles together outside to get the grit off them. She'd remind him that his *mamm* had warned him several times to clean his shoes after he'd been down at the shore.

Tying her bonnet under her chin and grabbing her scarf and mittens, Kirsten rushed through the house. It was empty, and the front door was ajar, letting in the cold air. Excited voices could be heard from the yard.

"Don't leave without me," she called as she closed the door and walked to the open wagon. The only available space was on the seat next to Mark. The teens and Theo were sprawled in the back, Daryn's feet hanging over the side of the wagon.

"We won't!" said Theo and Daryn at the same time

while Mark motioned with a grin for her to climb up and then offered his hand.

Her younger cousin added, "*Komm mol!* Time's a-wastin'."

Kirsten laughed with everyone at Theo's spot-on impression of Mark.

"This had better be fun," Daryn said. "I hope there's something other than old junk. That will be boring."

"It won't be boring," she replied.

"Gut." He glanced at Janelle. "We'll make sure it isn't boring. I hate boring."

Hoping they weren't planning any antics in Shushan, Kirsten reached for Mark's hand while she put her foot up to climb into the wagon. She smiled when Mark aimed a feigned frown at Theo as he repeated his impression of Mark. That seemed to delight the boy more.

She released Mark's fingers as she sat beside him and pulled a heavy, wool blanket over her knees. The flurry of succulent sensations emanating from his touch was delightful, but she refused to let herself be distracted. The outing today was for the younger ones. She couldn't allow her attention to be drawn away from them. Like Mark, she didn't want to believe his brother was mixed up with the vandals, but until that was certain, engaging the kids and listening to them was more important.

How many times would she have to repeat that to herself before she began to believe it?

The small town of Shushan sat in a pocket at the head of the bay. It was bisected by a bridge that spanned the narrow waterway. Shops edged both sides of the through street. A marina was set in the shadow of the bridge, crowded with small fishing boats. Most were about the size of Greeley's, but they hadn't been painted with insults.

"Shushan is an odd name, ain't so?" Mark asked as they drove past the bright green Welcome to Shushan sign at the edge of the village.

"It's from the Bible." Kirsten wrapped her arms around herself.

He understood her reaction. The open wagon was much colder than a buggy would have been. Handing her another blanket to settle over her knees, he said, "I know. It was the palace of the Persian king who was the husband of Queen Esther. Shushan is an old Persian word."

"Meaning lilies." She smiled. "I saw plenty of daylilies around town this summer, so it's named appropriately."

"I still say it's an odd name for a fishing village. Why didn't they name it Codville or something like that?"

"How about Flounderland?" asked Theo as he folded his arms on their seat.

"Or Haddocktown?" suggested Daryn.

"No, I've got it," Kirsten said. "They should have called it The Plaice." When Mark regarded her with confusion, she said, "Plaice like the fish. Not Place like place."

"Huh?" Theo grumbled. "I don't get it."

"Plaice," she said, then spelled the name of the fish that was caught off Prince Edward Island shores.

"That's silly," her younger cousin stated.

"Or that may be why," Kirsten said in order to halt Janelle's retort, "they decided to name it Shushan Bay."

Mark murmured, "I think calling the town The Plaice is clever, Kirsten."

"Not if someone has to spell the name all the time."

"True." He slowed as they neared where the shore road intersected the main street. "Which way?"

"To the left. I like the thrift store over there best."

They waited for several vehicles to go by, then Mark turned the wagon onto the main road leading west toward Charlottetown. The shops were set up in an interesting mix of buildings of various ages and styles. Some looked as if they'd been houses. A whole section was concrete with a parking lot in front. He'd been told the clapboard buildings that once had stood there had burned in a spectacular fire twenty years ago.

"Right there," she said, pointing to the shop which had a display of sleds and snow shovels in front of it as well as boxes of Christmas decorations. The window display included two animated angels and a pair of deer made out of wire and white lights.

Before Mark could lash the reins to the hitching rail, the kids were clambering out of the rear. Kirsten checked to make sure Janelle had taken her purse with her and that Theo hadn't forgotten his hat. Sliding to the edge of the seat, she started to step down.

Her eyes got large when Mark held his hand up to her. She froze and stared into his face. He put a challenge into his cheeky grin, and she chuckled as she relaxed. *Gut*! She'd urged him to see the outing as something fun, and he was trying to do that.

Though she let him help her down, she pulled her hand away as soon as her toes touched the concrete. He sighed. Her touch had banished the frigid wind off the water and teased him to step closer to her. He wondered how he'd failed to notice how lush her ebony eyelashes were as they brushed her cheeks.

"Are you going to stand there staring into each other's eyes all day?" called Janelle from the other side of the wagon.

Kirsten blushed, and he hoped he wasn't blushing too. He didn't look at her as he pulled up his scarf while she scurried around the wagon away from him. When she slowed, he guessed she didn't want to look like a kid caught with her fingers in the cookie jar. Would her kiss be as sweet as a snickerdoodle?

For once, he didn't shove that thought aside. He relished it. Her soft lips might be hidden beneath her knitted scarf, but he could recreate their curves. He'd admired them so many times their image was as clear in his mind as the traffic along the street.

"Komm mol," Theo said with a chuckle, halting Mark's thoughts before they could lead him further in the wrong direction. Not wrong-wrong, but wrong for this time and place. "Time's a-wastin' as you always say, ain't so, Mark?"

"I don't think I say it that often."

Daryn laughed. "Anytime you want to get someone else to start working."

He chuckled along with the boys, but his gaze followed Kirsten to the shop door. He'd been foolish to get lost in musing about his yearnings. Maybe that wasn't such a bad thing. He was beginning to wonder if being a fool at times was the smartest thing he could do.

Chapter Nine

By the time she'd reached the shop door, Kirsten had herself composed enough she could hide her reaction when Mark held the door, his arm brushing against her shoulder. Inside her, a brass marching band was playing an exultant tune.

She was saved from having to say much when the kids and Mark scattered through the store. She remained near the front while comforting Christmas music played from overhead speakers. Taking a deep breath, she walked in the direction of women's clothing. *Aenti* Helga's purse was falling apart. Maybe she could find one in excellent shape.

Kirsten looked down each row for purses. When she saw a familiar face, she smiled and went between the racks of clothing to greet her friend and coworker at Sea Gull Holiday Cottages, Gail Segal. While she and Gail had worked side by side in the half-dozen cottages during the summer, they'd talked about everything and anything. Kirsten suspected she knew more about Gail's five *kins-kinder* than she did about her own cousins.

"Good morning, Gail," she said.

Gail smiled. Her graying brown hair was in a bun

that was far looser than Kirsten wore beneath her *kapp*. Her round face was the perfect complement to her round form. She was the epitome of a loving *grossmammi*. "Hi, Kirsten. How are things going with your new company?"

"Getting better." She wasn't going to fill Gail's ears with the ups and downs of running a new company. "How are things with you?"

"Busy with the holidays coming up." She paused, then said, "I was going to stop by your house to talk to you."

"About what?"

Reaching into her purse, Gail pulled out a key ring with the familiar logo for the Sea Gull Holiday Cottages. "I was wrong when I told you that Lulu would open the cottages in the spring. Instead, she's decided to sell the resort. She asked me to find someone to fix them up so she'll get a better price. I can't do it because we're heading south for the winter."

"You're going to retire?" She tried to ignore the cramp in her stomach. She'd been depending on her job at the cottages in the spring to supplement her income from her cleaning business.

"I said I'd stay as long as Lulu needs me." One side of her mouth tilted in an ironic smile. "I guess I'm not staying quite that long, but I was hoping you could oversee the repairs and find someone to help. I hear the Amish are great builders."

Kirsten took the keys. "I'm sure I can find someone who has time over the winter to help. Do you have any idea what Lulu wants to spend?"

Gail smiled again as she named a generous figure. "I hope that helps you find someone."

"It should."

"It's good seeing you. Are you with the other Amish folks who came in?"

"*Ja*. Two of the younger ones are my cousins, and the other two are friends."

Friend seemed a peculiar word to use to describe Mark, but she wasn't going to examine that closer. Instead she accepted Gail's thanks and continued along the row. She wondered whom she should contact first about the job. It had to be someone she'd enjoy working with because it was clear that project was now completely in her hands. In addition, she knew what Lulu would expect. She would ask around to see who might be interested in taking on the job. She'd ask whoever it was to let Theo help. It would be a *gut* way for her cousin to learn some skills neither she nor his *mamm* could teach him.

Smiling again, Kirsten found purses hanging from a rack at the end of the row. A quick look told her there was nothing there she wanted for her *aenti*. Either the color or the fabric or the style was wrong.

"Look what I found." Theo's eyes glowed with excitement as he held up a pair of ice skates. "They're brandnew, Kirsten."

"In your size?"

"I'll grow into them."

She smiled. "And out of them as well, at the rate you're growing." She tilted the tag. "A *gut* price. They're a great find, Theo."

He beamed at her praise. "I can't wait to skate on the bay."

"The ice may be rippled from the tides."

"My farm pond isn't as big," said Mark as he came to stand beside the boy, "but it might be smoother. You could set up a hockey rink there. Daryn will be glad to help. He loves hockey, too."

"*Everyone* loves hockey," Theo said before going to

find Daryn who was looking at tools on the other side of the store.

"You're right about finding bargains," Mark said as he walked with her toward the kitchenware section. "He's thrilled with those skates."

"That's the fun of thrift stores. You never know what you'll find." She paused in front of the sign painted red and green and splashed with glitter. The letters on it read, What Does Christmas Mean to You?

"Do you have an answer?" he asked.

"I do have one," she said. "How about you?"

"I've got one, and I'll tell you mine if you'll tell me yours."

She laughed. "On the count of three. One, two, three—"

Together, they said, "Family."

His brows rose. "I didn't think you'd say that."

"Why not?"

"You don't live with your own family." His brow puckered. "I don't even know if you have any brothers and sisters."

"I don't."

"Are your parents living?"

"Ja."

"You're in Prince Edward Island, and they're in Ontario, or so I assume."

"I offered to help my *onkel* and his family get settled. When he died, I stayed on to help." It was the story she'd told everyone who'd asked. Everyone had accepted it.

Mark seemed to as well because he changed the subject as they continued to shop. A half hour later, they came out of the shop with several bags. In addition to Theo's skates, he and Daryn had found hockey sticks in *gut* condition, and Janelle had stocked up on the romance novels she loved. While Kirsten hadn't found a purse for her *aenti*, she'd picked up practically new cookie sheets and found a large Dutch oven. *Aenti* Helga would be pleased because it had a glass lid. Even Mark had bought something. He'd discovered a pair of work boots that looked as if they'd never been worn.

A diner across the street seemed convenient for lunch. While they waited for the traffic to clear, the kids talked about what they planned to eat. Kirsten gave Mark a grin when Theo acted as if he hadn't eaten a huge breakfast that morning after chores. Her grin broadened into a smile when Mark squeezed her hand and winked. The warmth spreading through her had nothing to do with the sun overhead.

They had to wait a few minutes for a table, but soon were seated in a booth near the back. Sitting between Mark and Theo gave Kirsten a view of the interior of the diner and the cars going by outside. Under her feet, a low nap carpet had given up its original color, but the dark wood top of the table was immaculate. Pictures of the Island decorated the walls covered with blue and green striped wallpaper. A Canadian flag with its scarlet maple leaf hung over the curved lunch counter next to a provincial flag displaying oak trees and an elongated lion.

The dark-haired waitress wore a red-and-white checkered apron. Whether it was intended to match the colors along the edges of the Prince Edward Island flag or not, the brightly colored apron accented the woman's cheery smile as she handed them menus.

When Theo ordered the largest burger along with poutine and onion rings and an extra-large chocolate shake, Kirsten hoped she had enough to pay for it along with her smaller burger and regular fries and Janelle's chicken sandwich. She reached for her purse to check while the waitress took the Yutzys' orders.

She must not have been as surreptitious as she'd hoped because Mark said, "Go ahead and order what you want, Daryn. Everyone's meal is on me today."

Beneath Daryn's eager order that matched Theo's but added an order of mozzarella sticks, Kirsten said, "You don't have to pay for us."

"I'm glad to treat everyone. My potato money came in yesterday."

She was about to remonstrate further, but then saw the gleam in his eyes. Not pride, but satisfaction at having tackled a tough job and seen it through to the end.

"Danki," she said as her cousins echoed her after the waitress took their orders to the kitchen that was visible through a doorway.

Mark waved aside their words. "I should be the one thanking you. I had no idea going to a used junk shop was so much fun."

"A *thrift* shop," she corrected with a laugh she was glad didn't sound strained. "Some people in Ontario call them 'charity shops,' but it doesn't matter what you call them as long as you don't label them junk shops. That sounds rude."

Daryn folded his arms on the table and grinned. "That's because my big brother is a snob."

Mark heard a sharp intake of breath. His? As he glanced around the table, he saw he wasn't the only one shocked by how his youngest brother had described him.

Kirsten put a hand on his hand balanced on his knee. She gave it a gentle squeeze. To console him in the wake of his brother's outburst? Or was she reminding him not to retort to Daryn?

Slipping his other hand atop hers, he didn't let her slide it away. He appreciated her gentle touch more than he could explain.

Daryn's eyes were wide. "I didn't mean it as an insult, Mark."

"Just as a fact?"

"Well...*ja*." His brother shifted on the bench. "You know you want things exactly as you want them. You can't be shaken from your opinions. I'm sixteen, and if I want to buy a buggy with my share of the potato profits, I should be able to."

"That's not a conversation we should be having now." He didn't want to accuse Daryn of bringing up the subject that had strained their dinner conversation last night after Mark had told his brother that the potato payment had come in. Daryn had been thrilled his share of the money was more than he'd ever possessed in his life, and he announced he was going to use most of it to buy a refurbished buggy he'd heard was for sale on the other side of Shushan.

"Why not?"

"This is a lunch with our friends. We shouldn't be talking money."

Daryn glanced at Janelle and got an encouraging smile in return. Did his brother want the buggy to bring her home from youth events? Kirsten wouldn't be happy about that. Her cousin was too young to get serious about any boy. Daryn wasn't old enough to have a relationship either.

"It's *my* money," his brother retorted. "You told me not to waste it, and I'm not going to. I'm investing in my future. I thought you'd be happy that I'm doing the best I can. How many times have you said that the only standards worth having are high ones?"

"That doesn't mean I'm a snob. It means I'm dedicated to doing my best."

"When that dedication means you think nobody else can do as well as you can, that's being a snob."

This time, Daryn didn't shift his gaze. His brother was speaking from the heart. Had he been too tough on the boy? Every time that question had popped into his head, he'd silenced it by reminding himself he didn't ask more of Daryn than of himself.

Theo broke the tense silence when he said, "Here comes our food!"

Mark reached for the dispenser to pass around napkins to each of them. As Kirsten accepted one, he saw the sympathy in her eyes. He let the conversation flow around him as if he were a rock in a sparkling stream. Kirsten didn't say much either, and he felt awful that his disagreement with Daryn had ruined her day. When, after they'd eaten and he'd paid, Janelle suggested they visit the other thrift store in Shushan, Kirsten's nod showed a lack of interest.

As soon as the others were hurrying along the street toward the second thrift store, Mark said, "I'm sorry about what happened in the diner."

"You don't have to apologize. I've had similar discussions with Janelle. Daryn will come around to understanding that buying a buggy is silly when he plans to return to Ontario."

"If he goes…"

Her eyes widened as wisps of her dark hair were whipped about by the wind coming over the bridge ahead of them. "He's not going home?"

"I get the feeling he doesn't want to. Last night, he said he'd never earn so much money if he works in the woodshop." He stepped around a puddle of slush and onto the bridge. "He doesn't know where he wants to be." Shaking his head, he added, "He's one mixed-up kid."

"Most of us are at sixteen. Our futures lay in front of us, and we could do or be anything we wanted to be. With infinite choices, it's not easy to see the path God has already created for us. We don't want to accept that the easy path—the one with God's blessings—is what we should choose when there are so many other ways and things calling to us."

"I've tried talking to him about things that interest him, as you suggested."

"How's that going? Have you seen changes in him?"

"Tiny ones. He's showing his sense of humor more, and he's not rushing out of the house after supper every night. Some nights, he doesn't go out at all."

"That's odd."

He paused and faced her. "What's odd?"

"Theo's been going out every evening. I've assumed he was with Daryn and his friends."

"He may be with the other boys even when Daryn's not."

She put one hand on the rail not far from his. As a car went over the bridge, the metal vibrated beneath his palm. He looked at where her gloved hand was less than a finger's breadth from his. The sensations that had spiraled through him when she put her hand on his in sympathy came awake again. If he took a half step forward, his arms could enfold her and draw her to him. A frisson that had nothing to do with the cold went shimmying down his spine. Until his farm's future was secure, he couldn't include anyone else.

"I guess I should be grateful," she said, drawing her hand away as if privy to his thoughts. She clasped her hands together. "Theo is no longer dragging himself around the house, and his steps have gotten lighter in the past few weeks." As she continued along the bridge, he hurried to keep up, though it took it all his strength not to sweep her into his arms. She added as he caught up with her, "*Aenti* Helga isn't happy when Theo heads out to meet the other boys after dark. He's twelve. She's concerned he may not paying enough attention at school."

"Theo's old enough to know the importance about being in bed early on a school night, ain't so?"

He could see that his comment had astonished her, and he understood when she said, "You are right, and I want Theo to make *gut* decisions for himself, not to follow blindly after his friends."

"But he's twelve."

"I'm not sure what you mean."

"At twelve, every boy believes he could become a superhero if the situation demanded it, and at the same time, he's afraid he'll be the only one who won't grow up to have an adult's superpowers."

She laughed. "Adult superpowers?"

"Look at it from his point of view. Adults make decisions. They have jobs that pay them. Theo is dependent upon you. I doubt there's a time in a boy's life more baffling than when he's twelve."

"And in a man's life?"

He chuckled. "*That* is a whole other subject. Let's stick to the current problem."

"The best idea I've heard." She smiled, and that warmth enveloped him again.

He savored it while he could.

Chapter Ten

"She's not coming."

Mark flinched and looked over his shoulder as he heard his brother's matter-of-fact voice from the other side of the dining room, but recovered enough to ask, "Who are you talking about?"

"Kirsten. You're watching for her, ain't so?"

"Not really."

Daryn chuckled as he leaned on the half wall in the kitchen. The plaster had been stripped from it, leaving broken strips of lath and dust. "I can't imagine why else you'd spend the past five minutes staring out the window. She's at Sea Gull Holiday Cottages today."

He nodded. When Kirsten had asked Daryn to work with her at the resort last week, Mark had been as surprised as his brother. More astonished when Daryn had agreed to help a couple of days each week. He wasn't sure whether his brother was more eager to make money or to spend time away from Mark. Either way, the boy was getting his wish. He didn't have time to be bored.

"If you're not looking for Kirsten," asked his brother, "then who?"

"I was just thinking."

"About her?"

He wondered when his brother had become so perceptive. He *had* been thinking about Kirsten, thinking about whether he should ask her to go with him to the benefit supper on Saturday night. If he didn't, he might be able to sit with her and her family. But he didn't want to sit with her family. He wanted time alone with her, and the best way to do that would be to have her ride to the benefit at the Shushan fire station with him. Each time he'd seen her in the past week and a half since they'd gone to the thrift stores, he'd considered asking her. Each time, he'd let the opportunity pass him by. He couldn't wait much longer. The benefit was only two nights away.

"How's it going getting those old wires out of the wall?" he asked his brother to change the subject.

This morning, he'd given Daryn the job of removing the electrical wiring from the kitchen walls. After they'd moved in, Mark had removed the fuse box in the cellar. As each room was redone, Mark wanted to get the wires out.

"Got most of them." He pointed to an outlet box in the wall. Not that one."

"Why not?"

"It's hot."

"Impossible." Mark frowned. "I pulled out the fuse box in the spring. There shouldn't be live power anywhere in the house."

"See for yourself." He handed Mark the small gauge which plugged into an outlet. "Glad you insisted on this. If not, I'd have fried fingers."

Plugging it in, Mark stared in disbelief when he saw two of the three lights were green. "There shouldn't be any lights on."

"That's what I thought. How's it getting electricity?"

"I don't know, but I'm going to find out."

An hour later after tracing the wires in a convoluted path through the house, Mark and Daryn had checked every inch on both floors, looking in closets and cupboards. Getting two flashlights, Mark had sent Daryn to explore the cellar's corners while he had thrown the light across the joists to see if something was hidden between them. They'd found dust and cobwebs that had been spun since Mark had done a *gut* clean-out before he moved in at the beginning of the year.

By the time they returned to the first floor, they hadn't discovered where the wires connected to live power. The only other possibility was the attic. Mark remembered there had been old knob and tube wiring up there, but had thought it was disconnected.

He reached for the pull-down door to the attic and straightened out the ladder that dropped from it. Climbing up, he shivered. The old windows might be drafty but the attic had been well-insulated to keep the heat downstairs. It was as cold standing on the single piece of plywood by the ladder as if he'd been outdoors.

"Wow!" Daryn stepped up beside him, then edging over to balance on one of the ceiling joists. "It's freezing up here."

"Go and get your gloves and coat." He watched his brother, waiting for any reaction when he mentioned gloves.

"I'll be right back." He stepped down a couple of rungs, then called, "Do you want yours, too?"

"Ja."

His brother disappeared down the ladder, and Mark listened to his heavy footfalls as he ran to the stairs to the ground floor. In less than a minute, Daryn returned.

He'd put on his coat and gloves downstairs and held out Mark's to him.

Mark took his coat and pulled it on, glancing at his brother's hands. "Those are nice gloves."

"*Mamm* made them for me last winter." He held up his right hand and rolled down the glove's wrist. "See? She put my initials in here like I was a toddler."

"Be glad she didn't hook them to your coat sleeve with mitten clips." Mark didn't try to hide his relief at seeing the gloves. There had been nothing on the gloves he'd found to identify who owned or made them.

"You're right." Daryn grinned.

"Are those your only gloves?"

"Ja." His brows lowered. "Why are you asking?"

"I found some down on the beach. Black knit ones like you're wearing. They had red paint on them." When his brother didn't answer, Mark added, "Like the red graffiti on Greeley's boat."

Daryn's brows shot upward. "You thought those gloves were mine? That I'd vandalize a neighbor's boat?"

"I didn't want to think you'd done it."

He must not have sounded too convincing because Daryn snapped, "You always think the worst of me! What more do I have to do to show you that while I'm not a mini-Mark Yutzy, I'm not someone who'd vandalize a boat?"

"To be honest, I wasn't sure what to think when I found the gloves."

Daryn's jaw was so taut he had to grind out each word. "You could have asked me, Mark. Showed me the gloves and asked if they were mine."

"I knew one wasn't yours, because the paint on it suggested the person wearing it was using his left hand to spray the paint."

"I'm not left-handed."

"I know."

"So why didn't you ask me instead of stewing?"

Mark shook his head. "I was afraid you'd tell me one of the gloves was yours. *Daed* and *Mamm* asked me to keep you out of trouble, and—"

"You didn't want to let them down." Daryn's hands unfolded from tight fists. "I get it, but next time you think I'm part of a crime, give me a chance to defend myself before you convict me."

"I will." He felt as if he were the younger brother being admonished by a wiser, older brother. "I'm sorry, Daryn."

Daryn rubbed his hands together. "Enough talking. Let's get this done. Even bundled up, my hands and toes are freezing."

"This way." He moved toward the right where a collection of wires hooked to white ceramic knobs snaked up the wall. "Let's start over the kitchen."

Mark stumbled when Daryn grabbed his sleeve and gasped.

"What's wrong?" Mark asked.

"Look! Look over there!" He pointed to the far end of the attic. "A rafter over there is bowed."

"What? Let me see!" He clambered across the attic, taking care not to hit his head. "Where?"

"At the far end. See it?"

Mark knelt next to the third rafter from the gable. Scanning with his flashlight along it, he whistled a single, long note.

"You're right, Daryn. It's not straight. Let me chase down the wire and disconnect it while you get some sturdy boards and nail them to the rafter to support it."

"Can't."

Turning in the small space between the gable and the first rafter, he frowned at his brother. "Why not?"

"I have to go."

"Where?"

"I told Kirsten I'd help her this afternoon."

Ignoring the pinch of envy that his brother was going to spend time with Kirsten while Mark was stuck tracing wires, he said, "Don't forget to repair it tomorrow."

"I won't." He scrambled down the ladder.

Mark sighed, then focused on tracing the wire. It took him more than an hour, but he found a small fuse box hidden in the shadows amidst dusty spiderwebs at the peak of the roof. Why it had been put there where it was so difficult to access was a question he doubted would ever be answered. He worked with care to remove it and unhook the wires. Before he returned downstairs, he aimed his flashlight at the rest of the attic. He found two more fuse boxes, but only one was live. He disconnected that one as well, praying there would be no more surprises.

It was growing dark when Mark returned to the second floor. He was gratified as he closed the attic hatch. Though Daryn would be going up there tomorrow, he didn't want to leave it open overnight to let cold air flood into the house.

A hot shower got the insulation and dirt and clinging webs off and warmed him up. Dressing in clean clothes, he went to the kitchen and tested the outlet again. This time, no lights came on the tester. He straightened and yawned. Crawling around in the cellar and the attic was tiring work.

He had just entered the living room when he heard a knock. Someone had come into the yard and he hadn't seen them? He must have been more exhausted than he'd guessed. A big yawn emphasized that thought.

Pushing his damp hair out of his eyes and reminding himself to have Daryn cut his hair, Mark threw open the door. His heart came to life, thudding against his chest, when he saw Kirsten standing there. He noticed she wasn't alone before his gaze was captured by her eyes, the only part of her face visible above her red scarf. Exploring those dark depths would be foolhardy, he guessed. A man could get lost within them and never find his way out.

Or never *want to* find his way out.

"If you're not going to ask us in, big brother," Daryn said, tearing apart the silken thread, as strong as spider's but sweet, tying Mark's gaze to Kirsten's, "at least step out of the way before we freeze."

Mark's feet were unwieldy as he moved aside. Daryn and Janelle were with Kirsten. He greeted them, hoping he sounded somewhat normal.

"Daryn told us you were chasing wires through the walls," Kirsten said as she unwrapped her scarf and left it hanging around her shoulders. "That sounds like thirsty work."

"You've got no idea."

His brother chuckled. "Trust me. We do. We may not be crawling around in the attic, but we're taking out furniture and cleaning behind and under it. I suspect some of the furniture hasn't been moved in a hundred years. Dusty work."

"Thirsty work," Janelle said as she untied her bonnet and put it on the kitchen table.

"Did you find the fuse box?" Daryn asked.

"Found three." He outlined what he'd done upstairs.

"It's done, so you can get up there tomorrow and fix that rafter."

Daryn grinned. "That's for tomorrow. Today we brought something delicious to drink."

"Helga's root beer?" Mark asked.

Kirsten smiled. "I've been told it's addictive."

"For Daryn it is. I barely got a taste before he drank what Janelle brought over before."

"We'll make sure you get some more this time."

Glasses were on a shelf in the living room to keep them away from the dust. Janelle hurried in and collected four. She turned and collided with Daryn who was opening the two quarts of root beer.

The glasses wobbled in Janelle's hands. Mark grabbed them as he helped Daryn keep his grip on the bottles.

"I'm so sorry," Janelle said, her eyes brimming with tears. "*Danki*, Mark. You saved the day."

He heard his brother mutter something that sounded like, "Again." Mark decided not to react to Daryn's petulant comment.

Instead he took the glasses from Janelle and put them on a low table by the sofa, trying to pay no attention to the plaster dust covering the top. It was impossible. He reached for a cloth.

Kirsten halted him by putting her hand on his sleeve. "Don't! It'll spread through the air, and we'll end up with a coating on our root beer."

"True." He was amazed he could speak that single word when her touch sent fireworks erupting through his mind until his thoughts were cluttered with "oohs" and "aahs."

When she began to pour out the root beer, he watched her graceful motions and wondered how it was possible for her to dance without a single note of music. Each thing she did reminded him of the pictures in a book his sister, Hope, had brought home from the library and hidden under a mattress. The illustrations had been of a ballet dancer who acted as if gravity had no hold on her.

Odd, he hadn't thought about that book since Hope had returned it to the library and brought home a title she didn't need to hide from their parents. Yet, as he watched Kirsten, those photographs played through his mind. She might not be twirling about on her tiptoes, but he could imagine her dancing across an empty stage.

What are you thinking? Such thoughts about a plain woman were ridiculous. If she gleaned his thoughts, she might be insulted.

Daryn went to show Janelle the outlet box that had given them so much trouble. This was the time to ask Kirsten to go with him to the benefit, but the words stuck in his mouth.

"Aren't you thirsty?" she asked.

"Ja." He took a gulp of the root beer as he dropped to sit on the sofa. A puff of dust rose up around him, and he waved it aside.

Or tried to. He'd had no idea his palms could sweat so much on a cold afternoon. He rubbed them against his dark trousers until he realized he didn't want a line of dampness down the sides.

"Daryn is doing a *gut* job at the cottages," Kirsten said.

"I'm glad to hear he's working better for you than he did for me."

She smiled. "I'm not his sibling. It's easier to take orders from me."

"Something I'll keep in mind." He took another drink, a sip this time. "I'm still learning."

"That's *gut*. I am, too, with my business. I'm trying to make sure when I make an assumption and it turns out to be the wrong one, I don't make it again. Life is trial and error and try again, ain't so?"

"True. I learned that at my *daed*'s knee when he taught me about woodworking, and I went through that when I was developing the desk that changed my family's lives." He gave her a wry grin. "I never looked at life as being the same type of trial and error."

"It's something I realized a long time ago. We all make mistakes, Mark."

"I know, but that doesn't mean it's not irking when I do."

"I'll pass along what my *grossmammi* told me when I was about Theo's age. Be yourself and trust in God. She told me if I followed those two rules, I'd find my way through this world was much simpler."

"That's great advice, but haven't you noticed? It's not working for me."

When she put her hand on his sleeve, he was astonished before he was suffused with a warmth that somehow slipped from her fingers through several layers of fabric to burnish his skin. He wanted to savor the sensation, but her soft voice drew his attention to what she was saying.

"It hasn't worked for you, Mark, because you've been anything *but* yourself," she said with a gentle smile. "At least you haven't been since we met."

"I am just as you see me."

"*Ja*, you are what you've allowed me and the others to see, but that's not the real Mark Yutzy. Your cousins have told me about what you were like before that desk changed your life. You weren't focused on failure or success. Mattie told me how you got in trouble for putting the goats in the cow barn and leaving the cows out in the field. Who does that sound like?"

He chuckled. "Point well taken. Thanks for the help, Kirsten."

"Could you help me, too?" He thought he had his opening to ask her to the supper, but she hurried on to ask, "Will you check with Daryn about what he and Theo and the other boys do when they're out in the evening? It's too dark for them to play ball. I can't imagine they'd walk to Shushan after dark."

"Boys in groups aren't known for having the best judgment."

"That's why I'd like to know."

"I can ask, but I'm not sure he'll tell me."

She nodded and glanced toward the other room. "I appreciate you trying. Sometimes, life is one step forward and two back. Sometimes it's just two steps back."

"That's pretty pessimistic."

"It's an observation. Not pessimistic. Not optimistic." She hesitated, then said, "Daryn told me about your conversation about the gloves you found. I'm glad you cleared the air. I don't want you to give up on him."

"I haven't. I wouldn't be worrying about him if I'd given up on him."

"Does he know that?"

"That I haven't given up on him?" He shrugged.

"Don't you think it's time to let him know how concerned you are about him?"

"I've been trying. He seems to be more open."

She glanced toward the entry and the kitchen on the other side. "I wonder where the kids have gone." Pushing herself to her feet, she said, "Let me see what they're up to."

He stood, too. If he didn't say something, he might not get another chance. "There's a benefit supper on Saturday night."

"I know." She smiled again. "*Aenti* Helga has been helping with the planning, and she's going to be over-seeing the setup. It's so *wunderbaar* how many volun-teers have stepped forward. I'm one, and so are Janelle and Theo."

"So you're going?"

"Of course. Helping to pay for a premature new-born's grandparents to come to visit and assist is such a blessing for us all." She smiled. "*Aenti* Helga is bring-ing her hot and spicy brownies along with the last of the root beer."

"Hot and spicy brownies?" he asked, knowing he was letting himself get distracted, and he was okay with it. Too okay, he warned himself. If he hesitated too long...

"They have cinnamon and chili powder in them. De-licious."

"People must be shocked when they take a bite." Why was he talking about brownies instead of asking her to go to the benefit with him? He never would have described himself as someone who couldn't resolve a problem head-on.

Until now.

Kirsten's soft laugh caressed his ears. "We try to put out a sign to let people know, but often the sign disappears. Usually on purpose when someone wants to see someone else's reaction. The brownies are so yummy nobody has been too upset once they get over their surprise. Are you going to the benefit? If you are, I'll make sure I save a couple for you and Daryn so you can sample them."

"We are going."

"*Gut*. I'll see you there, I'm sure."

As she started to toward the kitchen turn, he called her name sharply.

Too sharply, because astonishment widened her eyes. "What's wrong, Mark?"

"Nothing. Can I ask you something?"

She shifted to face him. "Go ahead."

"How about you coming with me—" He hoped she didn't hear his gulp before he hurried to amend the invitation. "With me and Daryn. Come with us." He was making an utter mess of this. How did his cousins make asking a woman to join them for an evening look so simple?

They've had a lot more practice than you have, honesty reminded him.

A lot more practice?

He'd had pretty much zero. When his friends and the cousins his age had been flirting with girls at singings and frolics, he'd been closeted in the family's shop overseeing the expansion of the business. He'd worried more about the quality control of his desks than his ability to engage a girl in conversation. Instead of picking out a pretty girl and asking her to let him take her home, he'd been concentrating on getting *gut* cuts of wood to build those desks. At the time, it had seemed like the right choice.

Now he regretted not practicing when everyone would have expected him to be awkward. He would have learned how not to stumble over his words as he was and how to look a woman in the eyes when he asked her out.

He cleared his throat, and the question burst out of him as if it were a single word. "Would-you-go-to-the-benefit-supper-with-me-and-Daryn?"

For what seemed like an eternity, she remained silent. It couldn't have been more than a few seconds.

Then she said, "*Danki*, but no."

He felt his mouth drop open. He should close it, but he seemed to have forgotten how.

No?

Of all the scenarios he'd played out in his mind to prepare for this moment, he'd hadn't imagined she'd say no. Did she want to be asked in a nicer way? His invitation had been sincere, though clumsy.

Somehow, he puffed out, "No?"

She gave him what he thought was a pitying smile. Why not? He was a pitiful mess.

"I told *Aenti* Helga I'd go with her early to help with setup. I'll see you there."

Then she was gone, leaving him alone to face the truth. He hadn't expected the first thing he might fail at in his life was convincing Kirsten to spend an evening with him.

By 3:00 a.m. the next morning, Kirsten gave up trying to sleep. No matter how she arranged her pillow or the sheets beneath the quilt, she couldn't fall asleep. The wind, for once, wasn't blowing off the bay to buffet the house, and the ice beginning to form on the water silenced the hushed motions of the water. Her thoughts had drifted off a couple of times, but then something jerked her awake as if someone had shouted in her ear. She stared up at the slanted ceiling and tried to catch her breath.

It wasn't a nebulous something that woke her. It was the memory of how her conversation with Mark had ended the previous afternoon. She'd fled from his house, dragging a protesting Janelle with her. No matter how many times Janelle asked what was wrong, Kirsten hadn't replied.

How could she admit she didn't trust herself? Going

with Mark to the benefit—and, oh, how she wanted to go with him—might be the first step toward a deeper relationship. She didn't want to fall in love with him and have him walk away as others had. No matter how often her heart pleaded with her to believe he wasn't like Nolan, Loyal and Hans, her brain whispered that her heart had told her the same thing about each of them.

And had been so wrong.

Saying no to Mark's invitation had been the right thing to do. She'd set a policy of not getting involved with their clients on a personal basis.

You meant getting involved with Englisch *clients.*

She couldn't ignore her conscience, even when it was vexing.

"What's fair for the *Englisch* is fair for the plain folks," she whispered to the night.

Sadly, the night didn't offer any *gut* advice.

Chapter Eleven

He needed *gut* advice.

From whom?

Frustration ate at Mark as he tossed another length of discarded wire he'd pulled out of the wall onto a pile in one corner of the barn, then leaned against the door. He yawned, fighting his exhaustion from too many hours of working on the house. Maybe if he'd had more sleep last night, he'd be able to think. He hadn't realized how accustomed he'd become to sharing his concerns with Kirsten and listening to her common sense. Now… It wasn't as if he could head over to her *aenti*'s house. What could he say?

Apologize for asking her to go to the benefit with him?

Saying he was sorry he'd asked her would be a lie.

Beg her to reconsider?

That wasn't going to happen. It wasn't a matter of *hochmut*. It was a matter of… Okay, it *was* a matter of *hochmut*.

With a groan, Mark pushed off from the barn door and walked toward the house. Should he go to the benefit? He could make a contribution and stay home. He didn't want to see who was taking her to the event at the firehouse. She must be going with someone else. She had mentioned she was going with her *aenti*, but what if she was going with another guy? Why else had she turned him down? He didn't want to think she simply didn't want to spend time with him. If that were so, why had she invited him along with the kids to visit the thrift stores in Shushan?

He had to stop tormenting himself with "what-ifs" and "maybes." He should look at this as a life lesson. *Learn, don't churn.* How many times had *Daed* said that when Mark was trying to master the basic skills in the woodshop? Mark had been frustrated then, too, stomping around and complaining of a sick stomach. *Daed* had patiently guided him through the steps Mark had been struggling to learn, and Mark's stomach had stopped churning with stress.

He paused as he reached the porch steps. Back then, he'd depended on *Daed* for *gut* advice. Whom could he ask? His cousins, Lucas and Juan Kuepfer, seemed to believe church Sunday afternoons had been arranged for them to flirt. Every Sunday evening, they took different girls home in their buggies. He had no idea how they did that. It was time for him to find out.

Mark didn't bother to hitch up his horse. Instead, he cut through his fields to where they connected with the Kuepfer farms that were side by side. Their houses were in as much need of work as his was, but he walked toward the barn where they milked their shared herd.

As he'd expected, the brothers were inside. They were tossing hay down from the loft to the ground floor. Shouting to each other, they kept up the spirited rivalry had started when Juan was born two years after Lucas.

"Busy?" Mark called up.

His cousins peered over the edge of the loft and grinned.

"Always," Juan said before walking toward the ladder.

They came down, grinning. Lucas and Juan were as unalike in personality as they were in appearance. Though thrilled to have the opportunity to work the lush, red soil of Prince Edward Island, Lucas, who had inherited his dark eyes and kohl-black hair from his Mexican *grossmammi*, was apt to be found with his nose in a book or magazine about farm equipment or varieties of potatoes and corn.

Not Juan, whose light brown hair was a few shades darker than the corn in the bin by the ladder. He seldom sat still for anything other than meals or church. He focused his time on the maintaining the equipment and tending to the animals on the farm. Each animal had been given a name, something he hadn't done in haste. He was determined that each cow or goat or chicken would have the name that suited her best. The only animal he hadn't named was the nasty goose that nipped at the seat of his trousers whenever he walked by. As he'd said more than once, the name of a creature like that one shouldn't be spoken aloud.

"How did you get past Christmas?" Juan asked as he peered out the door.

"Past Christmas?" Mark looked from one brother to the other. "We've got more than two weeks before Christmas."

"No, not Christmas the day."

Lucas grinned. "He's talking about Christmas the goose."

"Christmas?" he asked. "I thought you weren't going to name her."

"It's not a name," grumbled the younger man. "It's

a threat. If she rips another pair of my overalls, we're going to have roast goose for Christmas."

Mark laughed at his cousin's serious tone, before saying, "I could use some advice."

"We've got plenty of free advice," Lucas said. "Realize you get what you pay for."

"It's about women."

The brothers exchanged a glance before Juan said, "We've been wondering when you'd come by asking about that." He pulled himself up to sit on the edge of the bin. "Word is you and Kirsten Petersheim are walking out together."

"That word is wrong."

Lucas rested his elbow on a rung in the ladder. "Is that so?"

"Trust me. It's wrong."

Again the brothers looked at each other before Lucas asked, "So what can we help you with? If your dashing *gut* looks and smooth tongue didn't win her heart, I'm not sure what we can tell you."

Mark clenched his hands at his sides as the brothers laughed. He should too, but Lucas's teasing was as far from reality as Prince Edward Island was from the moon.

"So what's happened?" Juan asked.

He explained how he'd asked Kirsten to go to the benefit. "She said no."

"It sounds as if she has to be there early," Juan said.

"I could have taken her early."

Shaking his head, Lucas said, "If you want to walk out with Kirsten or any other woman, you've got to get her to notice you first. Have you made your interest clear?"

Had he? If he hadn't before, asking her to go with

him must have revealed he wanted to explore them being more than friends. "I think I have."

"Then it's time to go to Plan B." Juan jumped off the bin. "Nothing gets a woman more intrigued about a man than discovering that other women consider him a *gut* catch."

"I don't want to play games."

"It's all a game." Lucas chuckled. "It's fun to flirt when they flirt back. Women are okay with it, ain't so, Juan?"

His younger brother nodded. "As long as everyone understands it's just for fun, everyone has a *gut* time. Find a few willing girls and flirt with them. Focus on one at the benefit. If Kirsten sees, she might rethink her decision about letting you take her home."

"If she doesn't," Juan added, "then you'll still have some fun. What do you have to lose?"

Mark nodded, but didn't answer. Something felt wrong about their advice. Flirting, at least to him, felt like some sort of agreement that the two involved were considering a more serious relationship.

As long as everyone understands it's just for fun. Juan's words roiled through Mark's mind while he walked back to his farm. They continued to tumble chaotically when he drove into Shushan to order lumber to support the bowing rafter because neither he nor Daryn had been able to find a piece the right size in the barn.

As long as everyone understands it's just for fun. That, he decided as he drove into the parking lot at the hardware store, was the crux of the matter. Even if everyone understood at the beginning, what would happen if feelings changed?

Going into the hardware store, Mark placed his order and, picking up a small plastic basket, got nails and other small items for working on the house. He walked to the front to check out and found another customer in front of him.

The *Englisch* lady was buying a gallon of paint and insisted it be opened to make sure it was the color she wanted. The clerk, a woman with long, gray braids, complied. Both women were focused on checking the paint's color, so he put his basket on the end of the counter.

As he began to pull out the boxes and smaller items from his basket, he heard someone behind him ask, "It's awful, ain't so?"

Mark paused and looked over his shoulder. He recognized the red-haired woman behind him as Kirsten's friend, Aveline Lampel.

"What's awful?" he asked, setting on the counter a slip with the number of boards and sheets of drywall he wanted to buy written on it.

"The graffiti painted on more boats," Aveline said as the *Englisch* clerk hammered the top back onto the paint can.

His hand froze halfway between the basket and the counter. "More?"

Aveline nodded, her black bonnet bouncing on her head. She put her hand up to keep it from falling off as she said, "I heard three more boats were discovered this morning with the same words written on them."

"It was five," said the *Englisch* customer as she picked up her paint can. "Three in Shushan and two more in East Point."

"That's pretty far, ain't so?" he asked.

"About sixty kilometers." The *Englischer* turned toward the door. "Only an hour's drive."

An hour's drive in a car would be, he guessed, between three and four hours by buggy. Also the culprits needed more time to sneak out to where the boats were and paint them.

"That trip is too long for a plain person to go without someone noticing he's missing," Aveline said behind him.

He smiled at her, glad to have her confirm his thoughts. Every night, he waited to sleep until he'd heard Daryn return. Last night, Daryn had been in before ten o'clock.

"I heard about the spray paint on the boats in Shushan," the *Englisch* clerk said with a shake of her head that made her gray braids bounce on her shoulders. "I didn't hear about damage in East Point."

"These stories get bigger with each telling," Aveline said.

"It's a shame!" The clerk scanned each item and put it in a bag. "Those boats will have to be taken out of the water so the graffiti can be removed and the boats repainted. It won't be cheap, but at least it's almost winter."

"Why would that make a difference?" asked Aveline before Mark could.

"Many of the fishermen have their boats hauled out before the bay ices over. Doing that protects the boats and makes it easier for the owners to do maintenance so they're ready to get back to work as soon as the ice breaks up in the spring." She looked at the register and told Mark the total. "Someone needs to do something about these kids. They've got too much time on their hands."

"Are you sure kids are doing this?" Mark set his money on the counter and waited for change.

"Rumors—if you believe them—say that a trio of kids were seen not far from the marina last night. They were carrying something that looked like spray cans."

"So why didn't someone stop them?"

The *Englisch* woman chuckled as she handed him his

receipt and change. "That's why you can't trust rumors. They tell a great story but fall apart when you look at the details. I'm sure if someone had seen kids with spray cans at the marina, there would have been a hue and cry to halt them."

Mark took the bag and headed toward the door. The cold wind off the bay slapped him as he emerged, and he pulled up his scarf to protect the lower half of his face. He tugged his hat lower on his brow. His eyes, exposed to the wind, watered in protest.

He heard the door open behind him and glanced over his shoulder to see Aveline hurrying in his direction.

"Mark?" she called. "Do you have a minute to chat?"

His cousins' advice had been to practice his flirting. Here was his opportunity. He pushed the idea aside, though the glimmer in Aveline's eyes told him she wouldn't mind.

But he wouldn't use her, not even to get Kirsten's attention. He sighed silently, hating the bitter taste of failure in his mouth. It looked as if he'd better get used to it.

The benefit supper had been a rousing success with every chair snapped up as soon as it was empty. Plain people came from the three local districts, even the one ten kilometers away beyond Montague. *Englischers* joined the crowd, raving about the delicious food served. Everyone's favorites were the butter tarts flavored with maple syrup and *Aenti* Helga's hot and spicy brownies.

As the clock over the garage doors at the front of the firehouse struck nine, the meal was over, and many of the people had left. About a dozen stood in small groups, chatting before heading out into the cold. The air was heavy with the scent of impending snow, and a few lazy snowflakes drifted by the windows. It truly was beginning to feel like Christmas was coming.

Kirsten wiped the syrup off one of the plastic cloths spread across the tables in a merry array of patterns. Several were Christmas tablecloths to add to the festive atmosphere created by a pair of decorated trees the firefighters had set up in the back corners of the firehouse. Others had images of ships or kites or summery flowers scattered across them.

She tried not to look at where Mark stood with Aveline. The two of them had come to the benefit together. She'd been kept busy on the other side of the room, so she didn't have to devise something to say to them. Nobody had seemed to notice how choked her voice was as she struggled to swallow her tears. Knowing she had no one to blame but herself for turning down Mark's invitation, it hurt that he'd so quickly found someone else to bring. Someone she'd introduced him to.

Just as she'd introduced Nolan to her friend Gwendolyn and then been pushed aside when the two of them fell in love. Would she never learn? How easy it had been to chide Mark for failing to figure out how to deal with his brother! What a hypocrite she was! She couldn't even manage her traitorous heart which refused to listen to *gut* sense.

Aenti Helga came toward her, wiping her hands on a towel. "We're set in the kitchen. How are you doing?"

"Nearly done." She pointed with her chin to the other end of the long narrow space where a fire truck usually parked. A group of women were gathered there, sorting out dishes and trying to match them to their rightful owners. "Looks like Janelle is done, too."

"*Gut.*" Her *aenti* looked around the space. "Where's Theo?"

"I thought he was in the kitchen with you."

Aenti Helga shook her head. "No, he never came in. He said something about having supper with his friends, so I assumed he was out here."

"I never saw him." Her eyes widened as she saw a few teens were near where Janelle was working. Theo wasn't among them. "Do you think he left with his *Englisch* friends?"

"Without telling me?" *Aenti* Helga shook her head.

"He did tell you. He said he was going to eat with his friends." Kirsten scanned the room again, hoping her cousin would pop out, but her sinking heart told her she was being foolish.

"Mark may know where Daryn went, and wherever Daryn is, we'll find Theo."

No! she wanted to shout. She didn't want to have to talk to Mark when he was standing next to Aveline. She'd have to find something to say. No, she realized with a pulse of relief, she could ask him about Daryn's whereabouts. That way, she wouldn't have to reveal how hurt she was.

Kirsten pressed her dishcloth into her *aenti*'s trembling hands. "Check with the other boys and Janelle, *Aenti*, while I talk to Mark."

"Not until I talk to you first." Aveline strode toward her before Kirsten could take a single step. Her friend's face was tight with emotion.

"What's wrong?" asked Kirsten as her *aenti* rushed to check if Janelle had seen her brother or Daryn.

"Why did you tell me Mark Yutzy was just your friend?"

"Because he is," she said so her heart wouldn't lambaste her for not being honest.

"Does *he* know that?" Aveline grimaced. "Even

though he flirted with me yesterday like he really liked me, he didn't talk about anything but you through the whole meal. I might as well have been invisible."

She fought conflicting emotions. She couldn't help being thrilled that she was on Mark's mind. On the other hand, he had flirted with Aveline and asked her to come to the supper with him.

"I'm sorry," Kirsten said.

"It's not your fault." She sighed. "He's just another guy who wishes he was with someone other than me." Holding up her hand, she said, "You didn't ask to get invited to my pity party. Go and find your cousin."

Kirsten squeezed her friend's hand and then hurried to where Mark was pulling on his coat and looking around. For Aveline? Dark crescents underlined his eyes, and she wondered if he'd had as much trouble sleeping as she had.

"Mark, where's Daryn?" she asked without a greeting.

"Outside. Getting the buggy."

"Are you sure?"

His eyes narrowed. "*Ja.* Why?"

"Is Theo with him?"

"I don't know."

Pushing past him, Kirsten grabbed a shawl off the pile of coats on a chair by the door. It wasn't hers, but she flung it over her shoulders as she rushed outside. She saw Daryn on the other side of the parking lot.

"Is Theo with you?" she asked as soon as she reached him with Mark on her heels.

"No." He gestured toward the building. "He's right over there."

In disbelief and relief, Kirsten whirled to see the unmistakable silhouette of her cousin reaching for the door. She was about to go to the firehouse when Mark spoke.

"Was Theo with you earlier, Daryn?" he asked.

Shaking his head, his brother said, "No, I didn't see him all evening. I ate supper with Janelle and other kids. Theo wasn't with us." He frowned in concentration. "In fact, I can't remember the last time I've seen Theo."

"You mean you don't remember the last time you saw him tonight?" Kirsten asked.

"No, I mean I don't remember the last time I've seen him at all. Maybe when we went to Shushan that day?" He shrugged, his motion stiff in the cold. "I figured we'd be playing hockey, but he seems to be busy all the time."

Doing what? Where had he been? Thanking Daryn, she went inside, determined to get answers. If Theo hadn't been with Daryn... She halted inside the doorway when she saw *Aenti* Helga talking with Theo. Slipping off the shawl, she put it on the chair. She looked around just in time to see Aveline heading out the front door.

She waited for Mark to step past her to catch up with her friend. When he didn't, she asked, "Aren't you going, too? Aveline's leaving."

"She told me she's decided to go home with her *mamm*." His voice held no emotion.

"But she came with you."

"She did." He sighed. "I shouldn't have agreed when she asked if I'd like to ride with her."

"*She* asked *you* to come with her tonight?" Kirsten was confused.

"*Ja.* I saw her yesterday at the hardware store. She knows I used to make furniture, so she asked me how to fix a table that's been in her family for generations. I was giving her advice, and then she asked me. It shocked me."

"But she said you were flirting with her."

He shrugged. "She started flirting with me, and I…"

Putting her hands up to her ears, she said, "You don't need to say anything else. This is none of my business." She was proud of how serene her voice sounded. "Forget I asked."

He stepped in front of her as she turned to go. "Kirsten, listen. I don't know what Aveline told you about us."

Her heart contracted painfully when he said *us*, and it didn't include her. "She's my friend. She wouldn't be dishonest with me."

"I know." He ran his fingers backward through his hair, making it stand at weird angles. A motion she'd come to see signaled he was frustrated. "I didn't think I was flirting with her at the hardware store. Maybe I was."

She hesitated, recalling how Eldon had lambasted her for flirting with other men. She hadn't been sure—and still wasn't completely sure—what he'd meant when he'd chided her for talking with other men. If she was oblivious to what flirting was, couldn't Mark be, too?

When she didn't speak, Mark went on, "I'll have to talk to Lucas and Juan."

"Why?"

"They're the ones who said I should practice flirting."

"Why?" she asked again.

A flush rose up his face. "So I wouldn't make a fool of myself again like I did when I asked you to come with me tonight."

She threw up her hands. "Have you lost your mind, Mark Yutzy? Asking advice from your Kuepfer cousins about women?" She rolled her eyes as if she were no older than Janelle. "Don't you know plain women warn each other not to take their flirting seriously?"

"No." He looked abashed. "I didn't know that."

"You would if you weren't so focused on your farm and your brother—"

"Important things."

"I agree, but they shouldn't be the be-all and end-all of your life." She tried to batten down her anger, but it burst out. "Aveline is my friend, and I don't like how you treated her. It was no better than how Nolan treated me."

"Nolan?" His eyebrows rose with his bafflement. "Who's Nolan?"

She swallowed hard, now even more infuriated with herself than she was with him. Hadn't she learned to guard her words when she was upset? She'd known better than to mention her ex who'd used her to meet her best friend.

Instead of answering, she said, "What you did was heartless. Aveline was upset. You hurt her by not focusing on her when you'd agreed to have supper with her."

He shoved his hands into his pockets so hard she was astounded she didn't hear fabric ripping as his finger went straight through the bottoms. "I made a mistake. I was wrong, but I was annoyed when you turned me down. I don't like to fail at something."

"At anything, according to Daryn."

"I'm sorry. Is that what you want me to say?"

"No, what I want you to say is nothing." She turned on her heel and walked away before she said something she'd regret more than when she'd told him "no" when he asked her to let him bring her to the benefit.

Chapter Twelve

Kirsten paused when she realized she'd dusted the same rocking chair three times. With a frustrated groan, she rolled the cloth up in her hand.

Why couldn't she concentrate?

The answer was simple, but not one she wanted to hear. She was struggling not to let Mark Yutzy invade her mind. Just as she had for the past four days. Christmas was less than two weeks away, and she wished she could put up No Trespassing signs in her mind to keep Mark out. She'd tried, but then none of her thoughts could follow one another in logical order.

One thing was clear. He wasn't the man she'd thought he was. He was focused too much on himself and his successes and failures. The latter seemed to rule his thoughts. He was so determined to succeed at everything that he'd pushed his brother—and her—away.

Stop thinking about him! He's not your problem.

She had to do something physical to occupy her thoughts, but what? She'd already cleaned the whole house. If she rubbed a dusting cloth over that rocker one more time, it might begin to remove the varnish.

"Don't be silly," she muttered to herself.

But was that thought more ridiculous than the number of times she'd looked out the window to see if Mark was walking past on his way to the farm shop? Or how often she'd had to stop herself from flinging herself through the door and marching down the road to his farm?

And say what?

That she hadn't learned her lesson from four previous men who'd touched her heart, daring her to believe God had sent the right man to her. That she had begun to fall in love with Mark, though he could be the most inflexible man she'd ever met. That she had no idea how to fall *out* of love with him.

Kirsten fled from her thoughts as she locked up her client's house before driving home. She considered stopping by the holiday cottages, but she needed Daryn's help in moving more furniture before she could continue working there.

Nobody was home when she got there. Deciding to try—*again!*—to remove the tar from Theo's trousers, she went to retrieve them from the laundry room. She set them on the counter as the door opened.

"*Gute nammidaag, Aenti* Helga," Kirsten said.

"*Ach*, it is a *gut* afternoon." Her *aenti* set down her bag of cleaning supplies. With the December cold, leaving the liquids in a buggy wasn't wise. "What are you up to?"

Kirsten explained. "I figured I'd give one more attempt to getting the tar out of Theo's pants. If nothing works, I think I'll go to the hardware store. Maybe somebody there will be able to help."

"I thought you'd given up on that."

"You know me. I'm stubborn."

"Too stubborn for your own *gut*, if you ask me."

Aenti Helga softened her criticism with a smile. "Let me look at them."

"Go ahead." She stepped away from the counter.

Aenti Helga picked up the trousers by the waistband. Carrying them closer to a window, she poked at the black stain with a single fingernail. "It doesn't look like tar." She held it up and pressed her nose against the fabric. "It doesn't smell like tar."

Kirsten breathed a silent sigh of relief when she saw there wasn't a black smudge on her *aenti*'s nose. "Theo said it was tar, that he got it on him when he was helping a friend put on a new roof."

"Theo is pulling your leg."

"What?"

"You heard me. He's pulling your leg. If this is tar, I'll eat these trousers with ketchup."

"If it's not tar, what is it?"

The older woman scraped the fabric again and watched as tiny flakes broke off. "It looks like paint to me. Lots and lots of layers of paint."

"Paint?" she whispered. "Are you sure?"

"*Ja.* Stanley used to make a mess of his trousers when he was painting. I blotted the paint with turpentine before washing them." She shook her head. "That was when the paint was damp. To use enough turpentine to loosen this dried paint, you'll ruin the fabric." She went to the trash can and tossed them in. "Not even useful as rags."

Her *aenti* kept talking, but questions swirled through Kirsten's mind. Why had Theo insisted the mess on his trousers was tar? Had he thought she'd be less upset than if he got paint on his trousers? Or had he wanted to hide the black gunk was paint?

Sickness ached in her center as she thought of the

boats that had been spray-painted. That had been done with red paint, and the paint on Theo's trousers was black. Where had he gotten *black* paint on his trousers?

And how?

She'd talk to Daryn when they worked together next week again. Maybe he could help her.

Or you could go over to Mark's house and talk to him.

It would be the smart thing to do, but going there after the harsh words she'd fired at Mark at the benefit seemed impossible. She owed him an apology. Yet asking for forgiveness seemed impossible when he'd pushed her aside as other men had. Repairing their friendship could lead to more heartache.

Help me, Lord, she prayed. *Help me be brave enough to do what I must do.*

Mark came in from the mail and tossed a letter addressed to his brother onto the kitchen table. It skidded across the plastic tablecloth and fell to the floor, sending a cascade of dust and insulation with it. As he bent to pick it up, he sneezed.

"Too much plaster dust?" asked Daryn as he walked into the kitchen. He was in his stocking feet, and his little toe was sticking out of his left sock while his big toe peeked from his right one.

Saying nothing about torn socks or how Daryn should buy new ones with the money he'd gotten after the harvest, Mark replied, "I've cleaned this kitchen a dozen times, but there's still dust."

"You worry too much about unimportant things."

"Someone has to." Trying to put a careless sound in his voice, he asked, "Who else would do it?"

"You'll never know, big brother, because you've got to be in control of everything." Daryn didn't smile.

Why couldn't he, Mark wondered, be as at ease with his brother as Kirsten and her cousins were? It seemed as if, since that day in Shushan, he'd had to weigh every word, and even then, whatever he said got his brother's back up. Too many conversations had devolved into quarrels. Sometimes, it didn't get that far. Daryn walked out in the middle of what they were discussing, claiming he had somewhere else to be or someone else he had to talk to.

That left Mark alone, and he didn't want to be alone in the old, creaking house. He'd prided himself on being able to take care of himself and everyone around him. That *hochmut* had led to his mistakes. He wondered how he'd ever thought he could do everything himself.

God's in charge of the universe. He lets us handle the little, unimportant details. His *Daed* had said that with a smile when reminding someone that any problem could be overcome with prayer and faith.

"Janelle's coming over this afternoon," Daryn continued when Mark remained silent. "Maybe she can get the rest of it."

He looked at the ceiling joists that were visible now that the plaster was down. The wood was spotted with bits of gray rock wool insulation. As he watched, a single piece drifted down like dirty snow.

"It'd be a waste of her time to come in today," he said.

Daryn frowned. "Can't she clean the rest of the house?"

"The plaster dust is going everywhere. Ten minutes after she's done, it'll look just as bad."

"She'll have gotten rid of this layer." He pointed at the hardwood floors. "If we keep walking on it, we're going to wear the finish right off the floor."

"The finish is about gone already." Putting up his hands to forestall his brother's next point, he said, "Janelle can clean. I'll stop by the farm shop and let her know not to do the kitchen." He reached for his black wool hat and saw the dust clinging to it. "You should pick up your dirty clothes, especially the holey socks, off your bedroom floor before she comes over."

Daryn's face became gray, then reddened before he rushed up the stairs. If nothing else, having Kirsten's cousin come in to clean would persuade his brother to put his dirty clothes in his hamper.

Mark's lips tilted in a smile. A rusty smile because he couldn't remember if he'd smiled since the benefit. He hadn't had any reason to smile.

His smile drifted away as he thought of Kirsten. Every way he envisioned reaching out to her ended in making matters worse. There must be a way, but how?

Daryn's words tormented him. *You'll never know, big brother, because you've got to be in control of everything.*

Did he?

Show me how to hand control over to You, God. Show me the way to relinquish my need to manage everything... and live the life You've chosen for me.

Kirsten noticed Mark's buggy wasn't parked in front of his barn when she drove over to pick up Janelle who should have been done with cleaning the house by now. A trail marked where its wheels had cut through the low fuzz of snow covering the ground. Guilt ravaged her when she realized how relieved she was that she didn't have to face him when her feelings were so unsteady.

For the first time ever, Kirsten wished she was driving a car instead of a buggy. If she had a car, she could hit the horn to alert Janelle she was there. The cookies she'd mixed up earlier and put in the refrigerator must be ready to bake, so she didn't want to linger.

Who was she trying to fool? Herself? Ridiculous!

Why not admit that she wanted to get in and out of Mark's house before he came home? If she saw him, she didn't know what she'd say. Determined to make her visit as short as possible, she opened the door and stepped out of the buggy.

She went to the house, trying not to feel like an interloper. She considered knocking, but reminded herself that Mark must not be home. Opening the door, she peeked in.

Nobody was in sight.

Her nose wrinkled when she was met by the thick odor of dust and time. The kitchen was filled with ladders and tools were scattered across the countertop that was half ripped off. Overhead the ceiling was missing, and holes in the walls revealed where wires had been torn out. She hadn't realized the work on Mark's house was so extensive. No wonder he'd looked exhausted. He and Daryn must have been working on the renovations from morning until late into the night.

Sniffing again, she frowned. Where was the lemony scent of the cleanser she'd given Janelle to use today?

Kirsten walked toward the entry and the living room beyond it. All she could smell was plaster dust. A giggle tickled her ears as she reached the living room. Her eyes widened when she saw her cousin and Daryn sitting close to each other on the sofa. The teenagers were so enthralled with each other they must not have heard her come in. She cleared her throat.

Janelle and Daryn jumped to their feet, their arms entwined. Color splashed up their faces before they stepped back, leaving a couple of feet between them. Janelle clasped her hands behind her while Daryn seemed unsure what to do with his.

"I assume," Kirsten said, "this is why the house hasn't gotten more than a lick and a promise cleaning."

"Daryn says he'll help me, but…" Janelle's smile creased her face, wiping away her dismay.

And adding to Kirsten's. Didn't her cousin realize what damage she could do to her reputation? If someone else had come to the house before Kirsten had and found her and Daryn in an embrace, talk would whirl around the community.

"It's time to go." Kirsten didn't raise her voice or soften the steel in it.

Janelle was silent as she got her cleaning supplies, which hadn't been taken out of their basket, and went with Kirsten out of the house. Though Kirsten heard Daryn open the back door, she didn't look back. She urged her cousin to get in before she did the same.

As soon as they were on the road leading toward their house and away from the heavy clouds rising off the ocean, Kirsten said, "I know you're mad at me, but I don't want you to endure what I have. People will talk."

"Of course they will."

"When they talk about you—"

Janelle interrupted her again, this time with an unladylike snort. "What do I care if people talk about me? They talk about everyone. That's one thing I've learned at the farm shop. Yap, yap, yap about everyone else's business. A new *boppli* or a new buggy…it doesn't matter. If someone stubs their toe, half the Island has to comment on it."

"That's true, but your reputation—"

"Kirsten, stop trying to sound like *Mamm*."

"If I do, it's because I'm as worried about you as she is."

Janelle shook her head and rolled her eyes. "Nobody

worries like she does. She takes the smallest little worm of worry and turns it into a giant rattlesnake. If we're two seconds late getting home, she's sure we're dead by the side of a road. If someone announces there's a bumper crop of apples, she thinks we'll eat too many green ones and end up with a stomachache. If someone says it's going to rain, she thinks we should build an ark."

"That's true, but—"

"No buts, Kirsten," Janelle interrupted again. "You're my cousin, my friend, the sister I've never had. I want you to be those things, not my *mamm*."

Steering the horse around a slushy puddle, Kirsten tried a different tack.

"You know Daryn won't be here forever, ain't so?"

"So?"

She realized her cousin wasn't being antagonistic. Janelle was honestly curious why Kirsten was bothered by the fact Mark's brother was planning to return to Ontario.

"I don't want to see you," Kirsten replied, "get your heart broken when he leaves."

"Isn't that all the more reason for us to have fun now? He's a *gut* guy, Kirsten. He makes me giggle." Tears welled into her eyes. "Do you know how precious that is? Until I met Daryn, the last time I giggled—not laughed, but *giggled*—was before *Daed* died. Nobody but Daryn has been able to help me do that."

"I didn't realize."

"I know you didn't. No one has." She bowed her head and sighed. "Please don't say anything to *Mamm*. I don't want her to feel worse, though I don't know if she feels anything any longer."

"That's not true. She loves you and Theo as much as she ever has."

"I'm not talking about that. I'm talking about how she goes through each day on such an even scale I'd started to wonder if she misses *Daed*."

"She does. A lot."

Raising her head and meeting Kirsten's gaze with her pain-filled one, she whispered, "I wasn't sure until I heard her scold Theo after the benefit. She was furious. Like she used to get at us when *Daed* was alive. I miss that."

Kirsten turned the buggy into their yard and brought it to a stop. "I understand what you mean. I miss my parents, too."

"Then why are you still in Prince Edward Island?"

"You know why. To help your *mamm*."

Janelle jumped down and got the basket of supplies. Hefting it, she led the way to the house. Over her shoulder, she said, "Exactly why Daryn is here, only he's helping his brother. He's going to leave in a few months, and you will, too."

"Ja," she said as dismay swept over her. She hadn't given much thought to leaving Prince Edward Island. Where would she go? Home? She missed her parents, but not her self-loathing that she hadn't given them the *kins-kinder* they prayed for.

"Why shouldn't I enjoy this happiness?" Janelle put the basket on the counter. "Only God knows what's to come, and He brought Daryn into my life. Won't I be turning my back on God's plan if I'm unhappy when he gives me this chance to be happy? I know it's not forever." She donned a wry smile. "I don't want forever. I want to giggle. For an hour once or twice a week."

Kirsten almost said, "But…" She realized she couldn't debate Janelle's reasoning. It was logical and well-thought-out. Janelle was growing up, and her cousin was teaching *her*.

Reaching out, Janelle took Kirsten's hands. "Kirsten, nobody is guaranteed anything. I realized that when *Daed* died. Everything we'd planned was gone, but we could begin anew, knowing God is with us. Have you forgotten He is with you, too, Kirsten? Don't you remember how in Romans 8:31, Paul wrote, 'If God be for us, who can be against us?'"

"I remember."

"*Gut.* Then you know that each day we are given is a gift from God. Rejoice in it and be glad." Janelle dimpled. "I saw that on a plaque at the thrift shop, and it's stuck with me." She took the basket and walked into the laundry room on the far side of the kitchen.

Kirsten continued to stare at the door long after her cousin had closed it behind her. She paid no attention to the gusts rattling the windows. The storm was getting closer, but it was paltry compared to the tempest inside her.

Was it that simple? Should she be accepting each day as a precious gift from God and be thankful for it? Thankful from the depths of her scarred heart? Could she be happy? Simply happy as Janelle was with God's blessings?

As the thoughts roiled through her head, she got out the cookie dough and began to spoon it out onto the cookie sheets she'd set on the table before she'd left for Mark's. The thought of his name sent grief tumbling through her. She blinked back tears as she opened the oven and put the cookies inside. She pulled them right out, realizing she hadn't preheated the oven.

She went through the motions of baking the cookies, trying not to think about Mark. It was impossible. She'd made a mess of everything with him. He'd apologized for his mistakes. She hadn't.

The buzzer on the kitchen timer startled her. A gob of cookie dough fell off her spoon and hit the floor. Leaving it, she rushed to the stove and pulled out two trays of cookies. One of her fingers was scorched because she hadn't taken the time to make sure the pot holder would protect them. The trays dropped with a clang on the counter. She whirled to the sink and, tossing aside the pot holder, stuck her burned finger under cold water.

Tears seared her eyes. Not from the pain, but from her stupidity for hanging onto her anger and embarrassment for so long.

She'd heaped everyone in her past together, when the only one who'd truly betrayed her trust was Eldon. He'd asked her to be his wife. He'd picked the date for the wedding. He'd begun the planning…before he'd started making excuses to avoid her.

Loyal, Hans and Nolan had never made her promises. Not one of them had attempted to kiss her. They acted as if she were a *gut* friend, someone they enjoyed spending time with. Was that how they'd seen her? Someone whose company was pleasurable until they had the chance to go after what they really wanted? Or maybe, as Lucas and Juan had suggested to Mark, they were simply practicing flirting?

They'd been having fun, and so should she have been, relishing the time they shared. Instead, she'd become more and more adrift. She hadn't stopped to ask herself what she wanted. What she *really* wanted beyond her family's expectations that she'd marry.

Her life hadn't all been horrible. She'd let the drama in her life—the melodrama, to be honest—shadow everything *wunderbaar* that had happened at the same time…and since. Would she have come to Prince Edward Island if she'd married one of those men?

No.

Would she have been able to help her *aenti* and her cousins if she'd been settled and married?

No. She would have written supportive and loving notes, expressing her grief at her *onkel*'s passing, but she wouldn't have been able to help cook meals and offer them work while they struggled to deal with their grief.

She looked at the cookies waiting for her to frost them. She'd made more than she planned, even with setting aside dozens for the upcoming cookie exchange. She could take some to Mark and ask for his forgiveness in assuming he'd set out to hurt her friend.

And her.

Another blast of wind struck the house. A single glance outside revealed that the black line of clouds had moved closer. She'd better frost the cookies, pack them up and hurry to Mark's house before the storm kept her from messing things up more by delaying her apology.

Grabbing her spatula, she set to work.

Chapter Thirteen

$\backsim\!\!\!\sim$

Minutes after she left for Mark's farm, Kirsten considered returning home. The weather had taken a definite turn for the worse. The wind was as cold as if it came from the North Pole. Clouds scudded, thick and gray and threatening, as they consumed the last hints of blue sky and darkened the icebound bay. The trees whipped as the wind tore through their bare branches.

It was going to storm, but how soon? She hadn't lived long enough on the Island to anticipate its December moods. As she debated what to do, her buggy horse Chance kept stepping out with his firm clip-clop toward Mark's farm. She might as well drop off the cookies, offer her apology, which she prayed he'd accept, and then hurry home.

A gust hammered the buggy as she turned off the shore road into the Yutzys' yard. Chance shied, unhappy with the buffeting. Wanting to get him out of the nasty wind, she drove to the barn. Jumping out, she opened the door and led Chance inside. He shook his head, scattering bits of snow and ice that had caught in his mane.

Patting his neck, she said, "You'll be fine here, boy."

He gave her a look of disbelief when debris swirled

around his hooves, and a whistle from the eaves warned the wind was revving up even more.

"At least for now," she added. "Let me drop off these cookies. Then we'll head home, and you can ride out the storm in your nice, comfortable stall."

When the horse nodded his head, she smiled. She often wondered if he understood what she was saying. She took the boxes out of the buggy and walked into the strengthening wind, drawing the sliding barn door shut behind her. She tried to latch it, but the wind rocked it, and she couldn't close it while she tried to steady three boxes.

"I'll be right back," she said more to herself than the horse.

Rushing to the house, she winced as icy pellets scored her face. It wasn't snow, and it wasn't sleet, but a combination. She didn't bother to knock. She threw open the rear door and peered into the kitchen. "Mark? Daryn?"

No answer. She tried to ignore the disappointment coursing through her, because the longer she waited to make her apology, the more difficult she feared it was going to be. Hurrying in, she reached to close the door, but it fought her as the barn one had. She got it shut, then put the cookies on the kitchen table among the dusty tools.

She paused to draw in a breath that wasn't being snatched from her by the wind. An extra-strong gust of wind struck the house, and she heard creaks overhead and beneath her feet. She stiffened, praying the house wouldn't blow away with her in it.

She turned to go, then paused when she saw the shade on one of the windows flapping. Hurrying across the kitchen, she discovered the upper half of the window had slid down enough to let the wind in.

Reaching up as the shade draped down over her head onto her shoulders, she tried to close it. The cold wind pounded her cheeks, and more ice struck her. Gritting her teeth, she pushed harder. The window didn't move.

"Why are you hiding beneath my shade?" Mark asked from the other side of the room.

She shouldered the shade aside and looked out to see him grinning. "What does it look like? I'm trying to close your window."

His smile vanished. "Did it slide down again? Let me get it." He motioned for her to edge aside.

She did quickly. If she hadn't and they'd stood so close, she might have thrown her arms around him and invited him to kiss her. She stiffened at that thought.

Had he noticed the warmth building between them while they stood close? If so, no hint was in his voice as he said, "That should hold it. The wind isn't giving up, ain't so?"

"It wasn't so bad when I left home."

"Where's Chance?"

"In the barn. I drove the buggy in."

"*Gut* place for it." He paused as another gust battered the house, and his expression became grave. "Why are you here?"

"I was making cookies for Christmas, and I baked too many. I know Daryn likes cookies."

"Me, too." The brilliant blue pools of his eyes held powerful emotions in their depths.

If she dove in…

"Kirsten," he said, "I know you didn't come just to drop off cookies."

"I didn't." She dampened her dry lips. *Tell him!*

He arched his brows in a silent request to go on, then looked away.

She followed his gaze toward the windows. Icy snow was beginning to pile up on the outer sills. A groan of dismay slipped past her lips. She couldn't get snowed in here. The idea of being snowbound with Mark threw every corner of her mind into a tizzy. At the same time, her heart was whispering about how sweet it would be to spend the storm wrapped in Mark's arms.

"I owe—" She halted herself as the wind screeched like a wild thing along the eaves. The door strained against its hinges, and she shuddered. Before she could go on, a horrific crash came from below them.

Mark ran to the cellar door and flung it open. He grabbed a flashlight from a shelf at the top of the stairs. A *gut* idea! If an animal had gotten in, seeking a haven from the storm, the light would scare it away.

When she stepped toward him, he ordered, "Stay here."

She started to protest, but he headed down the stairs, the flashlight flickering on about halfway to the bottom. Looking around her, she ran to pick up a cast iron skillet from a stack of dishes in the entry. She didn't intend to strike a frightened animal with it, but banging on it with the ladle she'd found on the floor would send it fleeing.

She ran down the stairs in Mark's wake. He glanced back with an annoyed frown, but she didn't pause. Putting his finger to his lips, he sprayed the light around the cellar. Stone walls and dirt floors weren't inviting, and the ceiling was low, crisscrossed with pipes hung with dust-laden spiderwebs.

A motion came from near a disconnected, old coal furnace, and he aimed the flashlight at it. Two boys— *Englischers* by how they were dressed—stared before their gazes darted past them. Looking for an escape?

"You're cornered," Mark said. "There's a bulkhead behind the furnace, but the doors are warped and won't open. I cut off the lock after we moved in. After a few useless tries to open one of the doors, I gave up. You won't get out that way."

The boys didn't answer as they shifted from one foot to the other. The shorter boy's gaze seemed to zoom in on the heavy pan in Kirsten's hand. She put it on the step behind her and set the ladle in it. The clang of metal on metal was preternaturally loud.

"I'm waiting," Mark said as the noise echoed through the cellar.

The boys shared a fearful glance before the taller one, who was older, demanded, "For what?"

"For you to introduce yourselves. I figure it's the least you can do when you've invaded my house."

"We didn't invade," said the older boy. "We were invited in."

"Really? By whom?"

Both boys looked over their shoulders.

"By me," Theo answered.

Kirsten was dumbstruck when her younger cousin stepped out from behind the behemoth that once had warmed the house. Theo shook coal dust off his boots, but it coated his hair. Had the boys come into the house via an old coal chute? What were they thinking?

Then a more urgent question battered her brain: Why? Why would they risk coming into the cellar that way?

Because they didn't want to be seen.

Because they were planning mischief.

Because they knew what they were doing was wrong.

Then from the corner of her eye, she saw what the boys had been trying to hide. The taller *Englisch* boy held an aerosol paint can. He hid it behind him again.

These boys must be responsible for the vandalism. These boys and…

Her heart broke as she realized if Theo was with them now, he likely had been with them when the boats had been vandalized.

"What are you doing with these boys?" She didn't want to believe her sweet, young cousin had sprayed nasty sayings on their neighbors' boats.

"They're my friends."

"Why did you invite them here?" she asked. "It's not our house. It's Mark's."

Theo jutted his chin toward her with an angry expression Kirsten had never seen on his face. She yearned to throw her arms around him and cuddle him close as he reverted to the sweet *kind* she'd known.

"Who are your friends, Theo?" asked Mark.

She thought her cousin wouldn't answer; then Theo pointed to the taller boy. "That's Owen Lang."

"Owen Lang?" Mark frowned. "Aren't you the kid who threatened Mattie and Daisy at the farm shop before it opened?"

Kirsten gasped. "What are you talking about?"

"Before the shop opened, they tried to intimidate my cousin." He gave the boys a cold smile as he held out his hand in a silent order which the boys must have understood because they gave him their spray paint cans. Pointing to the stairs, he said, "That didn't work out too well, ain't so?"

"We didn't want that filthy, old building anyhow," Owen muttered, but walked up the stairs as if he owned the place.

The other boy and Mark followed after Mark put the spray cans on a dusty shelf.

Kirsten took Theo's arm, holding him back. She met

his defiant expression with her own. "Why are you with boys who threatened Mattie?"

"I told you." He wrenched his arm out of her grip. "They're my friends." He rushed up the steps.

Her head reeled with what she'd discovered. She picked up the pan and the ladle as she climbed out of the cellar. When she emerged into the kitchen, Mark gave her a sympathetic glance before his gaze riveted on the three boys again. She guessed he wanted to make sure they didn't retrieve their paint.

The back door opened as she was putting the dishes in the entry, and Daryn walked in. Snow swirled around him. He started to greet his brother, but clamped his lips closed when he saw the boys in the kitchen.

He pulled off his knit cap that wouldn't blow away in the wind. "Theo, I thought I told you to stay away from these guys."

With a frown, Theo said, "You're not the boss of me, Daryn Yutzy."

"Did you learn stupid things like that from them?"

Theo didn't answer, and the other two boys edged toward the door. They halted when the wind slammed the house.

Kirsten gripped the edge of the table as the floor vibrated under her feet. Could the old house survive the blizzard? Mark's face hardened when he looked out the nearest window. His expression when he turned to her told her none of them were going anywhere any time soon. The boys must have realized it, too, because they grew pale.

She was grateful for Mark's serenity in the face of such anger. It sanded the edges off what could have been an explosive situation. Watching him, she could tell he chose each word and every action with care, hoping to stop the boys from trying something stupid. His silence as he looked from one boy to the next was calculated. Telling him she was sorry for how she'd acted at the benefit no longer seemed like a frightful task. She *wanted* to apologize because she knew he would listen without judgment.

Now was not the time, however. She stayed mute while waiting for Mark to speak. This was his home, though it was their shared problem.

She was surprised Mark's next words were aimed at Daryn. "So these are your and Theo's friends? The ones you've been going out with in the evening?"

"Maybe Theo was with them," his brother said, "but I wasn't. Other than Theo, I haven't seen these guys in weeks."

"Theo said he was with you," Kirsten interjected.

Daryn's brows lowered, making him look more like his older brother than ever before. "Theo was lying. I don't hang around with punks and losers."

"Daryn," growled Mark. "I won't have you calling anyone names."

"They aren't names, Mark." He shoved his hands into his pockets. "That's what they are. Would you prefer I call them troublemakers or ruffians?"

"I'd prefer to know their names," Kirsten said, folding her hands in front of her. "Theo?"

"I told you. That one's Owen Lang. The other guy's Roddy Buckley."

"Hey!" the *Englisch* boys said at the same time before Roddy went on, "Why are you blabbing? What about our pledge to keep quiet about things?"

"Plain folks don't make pledges." Kirsten shifted her gaze from the two boys to her cousin. "Theo should have mentioned it to you."

"He should have!" Owen snarled. "Instead he ratted us out."

"Enough!" Mark's word snapped like a whip through the room. "You've wasted enough of our time quibbling about something that's not important." He didn't pause, ignoring Owen whose chest puffed out as he gathered in a deep breath to retort. "I want to know why you're in my house. Theo is welcome here, but I don't know you two. Were you planning to spray-paint my house like you did the boats?"

"You don't know what you're talking about, mister," Owen fired back.

"Maybe not, but would Constable Boulanger?"

At the mention of the officer of the Royal Canadian Mounted Police, all three boys became as gray as the sky barely visible through the swirling snow.

A sharp sound ricocheted through the house. Beside her, Theo put his hands over his ears and crouched as if the noise was painful.

It was.

Her ears ached from the concussion. What had happened?

Whatever it was had happened upstairs. The joists overhead trembled. Dust fell onto her bonnet and tumbled down its stiff sides.

"What was that?" cried one of the *Englischers*.

When Mark motioned for quiet, no one spoke as the wind howled around the eaves. Then the crash came again. Louder this time.

Mark raced out of the kitchen and up the stairs, still holding his flashlight. She hoped a tree hadn't been blown on the house. She and Mark were responsible for four kids in the midst of a blizzard. If the house wasn't safe…

Kirsten started to follow, then halted, unsure if the boys should be left alone in the kitchen. Would they be foolish enough to flee into the storm?

"Go," Daryn said from behind her. "Even these guys aren't witless enough to go outside now."

Giving the teen's shoulders a quick squeeze, she whispered, "Stay safe."

"I hope we can."

She hoped so, too, as she ran after Mark.

Mark raced toward the attic access, but he couldn't outrun his thoughts. What had Kirsten been about to say to him when they were interrupted by noise from the cellar? She'd brought cookies over, ignoring the impending storm. Were they just an excuse? Did she need to talk to him as much as he needed to talk to her?

Not seeing Kirsten these past four days had left a hole in his gut. After years of acting as if he didn't care about having a serious relationship, he'd messed up this one with Kirsten. More than messed up. He'd hurt her, and he was infuriated with himself.

Not now! Something was wrong up in the attic, and he had to find out what. He was opening the pull-down ladder to the attic when he heard footsteps behind him. He was about to shout over his shoulder, but recognized them as Kirsten's. Why hadn't she stayed with the boys in the kitchen?

He wanted to moan when he saw small drifts gathered on each step. Icy flakes swarmed like a million angry bees into the stairwell.

"There's got to be a hole in the roof," he said. "There's too much snow. It can't just be coming through the vents. Maybe that's what we heard. A part of the roof blowing off." He motioned her aside. "Wait here."

He didn't give her a chance to answer. Scrambling up the ladder, he grimaced when his shoes slid on the ice. He reached the top and stepped onto a sheet of plywood that had a couple inches of snow on it. He panned the flashlight across the underside of the roof.

"What do you see?" Kirsten's question came from right behind him. No surprise. He was about to urge her to go back downstairs when he saw a lighter space along the roof. Not large. Not yet. Two boards supporting the farthest rafters had broken into jagged pieces. The sheared-off rafters had dropped into the filthy insulation, sending it floating around the attic. He gasped as a section of shingles collapsed into the attic. As she climbed up to stand beside him, she gasped. "Is that a hole in the roof?"

He flashed the light toward the far end of the attic where snow blew in. "It is, and it's getting bigger."

He heard a warning groan from the other side of the attic. A rafter bowed toward the floor. Grabbing Kirsten, he shoved her down onto the plywood. When she cried out, he pressed down on top of her, his arms around his head.

A crack sounded like a powerful rifle. She moaned, and he swallowed his cry of pain as splinters flew around them, one slicing across his cheek.

"What's happened?" she cried.

"Another rafter just broke!" He had to shout because the roar of the storm was louder.

He raised his head and saw a wide hole on one side of the roof. A cloud of dust and debris was being batted down by the snow and ice.

Kirsten slipped out from beneath him. "You're bleeding."

She dabbed her apron against his right cheek beneath

his eye. A few centimeters higher… She shuddered, and he wrapped his arms around her as he'd wanted to so many times.

"I'm fine," he said, though he wasn't. Not really. "How about you?"

"I'm okay."

The house shook as another gust hammered it.

Grabbing her hand, Mark pulled her to the ladder. He guided her down so fast her feet slid on every step. He shut the door, but snow squeezed past its edges as they ran toward the stairs to the ground floor.

He looked at her and saw blood on the left sleeve of her black coat. Why hadn't she said she was hurt? Her sleeve had been sliced through, and slivers poked out of the wool around the hole like a black hedgehog. A splinter must have cut through the wool and into her arm. Gently he lowered her coat from her shoulders and examined the splinter in her arm.

"Shall I remove it?" he asked.

"Ja." Her voice was breathless. "Quickly please."

Mark took a deep breath after telling her to do the same. He heard her soft moan as he pulled the wood out. He pulled a handkerchief out of his pocket and tied it around her arm before lifting her coat over her shoulders.

"We'll get it cleaned and tended to…"

"It's bad, ain't so?"

"Your arm?"

Kirsten shook her head. "No, I mean the rafters."

"Bad. Very bad." He wouldn't be false with her. Taking her right hand, he raised it to his lips for a fleeting kiss. He yearned for a longer kiss, a kiss on her lips, but he led her down the stairs to the ground floor.

When they reached the kitchen, Daryn asked, "What did you find?"

"A mess! Daryn, I thought you fixed that rafter."

"I did!"

"Then why did it snap?"

"Is that what we heard?" Fear blossomed in his eyes.

"*Ja*, and it wasn't the only one." He had their attention. The boys looked confused as well as scared.

Daryn asked, "Another one broke?"

"Two more." As he said that, another ear-shattering creak erupted through the house followed by a heavy thud. "Three more."

"We have to go before the roof collapses." Kirsten pointed toward the door. The teens stared at her in disbelief until she clapped her hands. "Go!"

"Go where?" asked Owen.

"Outside!"

He hooked a thumb toward the window where the wind was hurling icy pellets in a cacophony of pings. "Are you crazy, lady?"

"Maybe," she answered, "but I'm not crazy enough to stay in a house that's caving in."

The boys exchanged a fearful glance, then Roddy said, "We can't go out there. It's a blizzard. You won't be able to see your hand in front of your face."

Mark turned to his brother. "How many times have you bragged you've found your way to the barn with your eyes shut because you were still asleep when we started chores?"

"It's just a saying. I could… I think…" He swallowed hard. "I'll do my best, Mark."

"That's all anyone can ask." He clapped his brother's shoulder. *"Komm mol."* For the *Englischers*, he repeated so they'd understand, "Let's go!"

Kirsten put her arm around Theo and moved toward the door. Daryn pulled on his coat, ready to lead the way.

The two *Englischers* didn't move.

"Let's go," Mark repeated, motioning with the flashlight, this time making it an order.

"I don't think going out in that storm is smart," Roddy said.

"But you think painting graffiti on someone else's property is smart?"

The boy subsided, his bravado wavering.

Owen scowled. "You don't tell us what to do!"

"I'm not trying to tell you anything but to get out before the whole house falls on top of you."

"You're not the boss of me," he snarled as Theo had earlier. Her cousin had the grace to look dismayed as he heard his words repeated.

Mark's answer was forestalled when another creak was followed by a sharp crack. The whole house trembled. The walls seemed to wobble in and out as if the house had sighed its final breath.

"*Komm mol*! We don't have time to argue." He threw open the door and stepped out into the blizzard, his arm around Kirsten and hers holding onto her cousin. Daryn edged around him, and Mark prayed the two *Englisch* boys would follow, so they wouldn't be crushed if the house fell in.

He prayed he wasn't making the worst mistake of his life. Six lives could be lost if he was wrong.

God, guide us to safety.

Chapter Fourteen

The storm was worse than Mark had guessed. He pushed everyone back inside, trying to ignore the terror on the kids' faces. Yanking open the cellar door, he pulled out a length of clothesline. He'd bought it months ago, but had been too busy working in the fields to install a clothesline.

Now he was glad he hadn't. The dangers of staying in the house were greater than the storm.

"Grab hold," he ordered the boys. "Wrap it around your arm so if you drop it when the wind hits you, you won't lose it." When the boys regarded him in confusion, he took one end, measured out two arms' length, and then twisted the next section around his forearm. Kirsten held up her arm, and he did the same for her, far enough away from him so they could walk without tripping over each other. He stuffed the flashlight in his pocket, knowing they soon could be depending on it. To the others, he bellowed, "Hurry!"

A strange rumbling from overhead sent the boys into overdrive. They lashed the rope around themselves. Daryn stepped forward, grasped the rope in front of

Mark and wrapped it around his waist, tying double knots. He glanced at the fierce storm and took a deep breath.

"Please pray that I can do this," Daryn said.

"Close your eyes and lead us to safety." Mark clapped his brother on the shoulder. "We'll be right behind you, and God is with us. Don't let go of the rope." He repeated the last to the others.

Kirsten had the rope wrapped around her hurt arm, and her other arm locked through her cousin's. Theo looked terrified, but his chin jutted with resolve. The *Englisch* boys at the end of the rope clung to each other, too. He hoped they'd work together and not slow them down as they went the fifty meters to the barn.

Daryn bent his head and took a single step into the storm. The snow swallowed him. Mark gulped hard. He'd known the blizzard was bad, but to see Daryn disappear... He gave a slight tug on the rope. He didn't want to pull his brother off his feet, but needed to be sure Daryn was still there. The rope remained taut.

Following in Daryn's footsteps, though the wind was blowing snow into the prints as soon as they were made, Mark wished he'd put on his scarf. His face was slashed by the icy crystals that flew past like bullets from a gun. The wind whistled against his ears, changing pitch each time he moved his head. Knowing it was a waste of time, he looked back. He saw the rope by his elbow and Kirsten's fingers.

A gust struck him hard. He dropped to one knee. The rope burned his fingers and tightened on his arm as Daryn kept moving forward. As he scrambled to his feet, Kirsten stumbled against him. He swept his free arm around her waist. His instinct was to turn her so her face would be protected against his shoulder. Then she wouldn't be able to walk in a straight line.

He sent up an urgent prayer. The same prayer he'd said when he realized Daryn's accusation was true. *Show me how to hand control over to You, God. Show me the way to relinquish my need to manage everything...and live the life You've chosen for me.* The prayer came from the depths of his heart, cracking the prison he'd created for it when success convinced him that he had to be in charge. He was doing what Kirsten had urged him to do. Trust Daryn.

Wanting to ask Kirsten if she and Theo were okay, Mark kept his mouth closed. The roaring wind would steal his words, and he didn't want the frigid air rushing down his throat.

Daryn halted, and Mark's gut clenched. Were they lost? If they followed their steps back to the house... He glanced down. The snow was halfway up his shins. The footprints behind him had already disappeared.

"Don't rush him," Kirsten whispered near his ear. Maybe she shouted. He couldn't tell with the screeching wind.

He breathed a sigh of relief when the rope in his hand grew taut again. Blinded by the storm, he tried to match Daryn's steps and directions. Once he went too far to the left and had to edge back so he was behind his younger brother again.

Then the blizzard's assault halted, and boards were beneath his feet. Mark kept slogging forward at the same pace, stepping around his brother who'd dropped to the floor, his head hanging and his breath ragged. He pulled the flashlight out of his pocket, turned it on and aimed it at the door.

As soon as he saw the last boy appear out of the storm, Mark sat on a nearby hay bale. He unwound the rope and let it fall to the floor.

"I'm sorry about stopping out there," Daryn said as he gulped in air. "Breaking a path through the snow is hard work."

"Ja." He put his hand on his brother's shoulder. "You did a great job, Daryn. You got us here."

His brother smiled as he hadn't since he'd come to Prince Edward Island. Mark realized Kirsten had been right when she told him to focus on what Daryn did well.

At the thought of her, he watched as she hugged Theo. She looked over the boy's head at him, and Mark chuckled.

"What's so funny?" she asked.

"Seeing you with white hair. Every part of you that was walking into the wind is white."

"You, too." She ran her fingers through his hair, shaking loose snow to fall onto his coat's shoulders.

He caught her wrist and stood. Without a word, he pulled her to him. His lips ached to touch hers. Cold billowed off her wool coat. That didn't matter because having her so close sent a wave of warmth through him. He curved his fingers along her face. Her eyes glowed as her lips parted.

"Look!" intruded a fearful shout from closer to the door.

Kirsten wanted to remain lost in the sweet fantasy of Mark's kiss. Then she heard frantic voices shouting, "What's going on?" and "Are you seeing this, too?"

Mark released her and ran toward the open door where the others had gathered. She looked out as he waved the flashlight side-to-side. All she could see was the blizzard. Then a slow, rumbling sound rolled toward them like the waves along the beach. A shadow moved.

The house.

It was moving.

How was that possible?

She never knew if she'd asked that question aloud because the rumble became the howl of a wounded beast as the shadow crumbled into itself and vanished. Swarming dust thrust itself through the blizzard.

Right toward the barn.

"Close the door!" she shouted.

Theo and Owen grabbed the door and slid it shut. Mark and the other *Englisch* boy rushed to hold it steady while Daryn locked it in place. They jumped as huge pieces of debris hit the wood. Dust swirled beneath the door and into the barn. Somewhere along the barn, glass splintered, and the shriek of the wind rose through the broken window.

"What happened?" whispered Theo.

"The house fell down." Kirsten hardly believed her own words.

The kids looked up as one when rubble hit the roof.

She put her hand on Chance's flank to calm him when he shifted. She unhitched the horse and led him into a stall next to where Mark's horse was watching the invasion of his barn with indifference.

"It'll be okay, boy," she said as she closed the stable door. The words were automatic, but she wondered if they were true.

Mark's home was gone. They were stuck in a barn in the middle of a blizzard that could go on for hours. How long would the flashlight last? They didn't have food, and the only blankets were the two in her buggy. They were sweaty from the hard walk across the yard, but that wouldn't last. If she turned on the buggy's heater, how long before the battery was drained?

An explosion brought shouts of alarm from the boys. Orange light filled the barn, and a wave of heat washed over them.

She ran to where Mark was looking out a window. A fireball rose into the sky, searing her eyes with its brightness. The wind grasped it, and for an appalling moment, she thought the storm was going to blow the fire at the barn. Then the flames swirled and dropped into the rubble that once had been Mark's house.

"Was that blast from the propane tanks?" she asked, aware that the kids were too terrorized to speak.

"*Ja*, and I've been thanking God they didn't rupture before we got inside the barn. If the wind had changed direction, we would have been toast." He faced her. "No need to look frightened. We're not in any danger from the propane tanks now. Everything is gone."

"I'm sorry, Mark."

"We are alive." He smiled. "God's grace guided us, and His hand on the storm kept us safe."

"No, I meant I'm sorry for what I said the night of the benefit." The words burst from her with the power of the debris being flung across the yard.

"I know you are." He gave her a sad smile. "What I don't know is why you assumed I wanted to hurt you and Aveline."

As she searched for an answer that wasn't a lie but didn't give him the sad list of her failed romantic relationships, Theo called her name.

"He needs you," Mark said.

How could she have labeled him coldhearted? She

owed him more apologies than she'd realized. But they would have to wait.

She walked to where her cousin huddled against the rear wheel of the buggy. Sitting beside him, she held out her arm, and Theo nestled close to her.

She wasn't surprised when he whispered, "I'm sorry, Kirsten."

"I know you are."

"They said we wouldn't get in trouble." He looked across the barn to where the two *Englisch* boys were pacing, determined to escape the minute the storm abated.

"They were wrong."

He gave a half whimper and pressed his head against her shoulder. "I thought it was going to be fun. I believed Roddy when he said the first boat, which was his *onkel*'s, was due to be painted anyhow. We had a *gut* time spraying that one with funny sayings."

"You used red paint on that boat, ain't so?"

"Ja."

"So how did you get *black* paint on your trousers?"

"Owen thought I should practice using a spray can before we painted the boat. He thought it was funny to spray me to show me how to do it." His voice quivered. "It was funny. At first. Then they wanted to do more. I tried to get out of it, but they said if I did, they'd tell the cops and blame it all on me."

She sighed. "You defended them in the house."

"They've been *gut* friends, and we've had *gut* fun." He lowered his head as he added, "Other than the painting the boats. It was wrong, and I was afraid of *Mamm* finding out."

"And being disappointed in you?"

He shook his head, his hair flapping into his eyes. "I

didn't want her to be hurt again. She's in so much pain from *Daed*'s death."

Though she almost said they all were, she kept her mouth closed. Theo needed to talk, and she must not interrupt.

"What do you think will happen now?" he asked.

She wouldn't lie to him, even to soothe him in the wake of escaping a collapsing, burning house. "The police will want to talk with you. They're going to ask you questions, and you've got to answer them truthfully. They'll want to know if the gloves Mark found belonged to you."

"Mark found gloves?" When she quickly explained, Theo said, "They belonged to Owen and Roddy. They said they were going to get rid of them so nobody could pin the graffiti on them." He hung his head. "That's when I began to suspect they weren't being honest with me."

"*Danki* for telling me that. You must do the same with the police. No hedging, no hemming and hawing, no half-truths. You've got to tell them the truth."

"Like in a court?"

"*Ja.*" She fought to quell the thought of her young cousin having to stand before a judge and jury to learn the cost for his crimes. No, not a jury, she reminded herself, because he was a minor. It would be a judge, and she prayed it wouldn't come to that.

"I don't want to go to jail."

Smoothing his wind-blown hair, she murmured, "Whatever happens, remember two things. One, tell the truth, even when those around you don't."

"You think they'll lie to the police?" He frowned at his *Englisch* friends who were sitting at the edge of the light.

"I don't know what they'll do." She smiled at him. "But I know you, Theodore Petersheim. You're a *gut* kid, and you know right from wrong."

He gave her a hopeful smile. "What's the second thing to remember?"

"Something you know already."

"What's that?"

She squeezed his shoulders. "No matter what happens, your family will be there to help you. We won't ever abandon you."

"Daed—"

"Do you think he would have left if God had given him the choice? God has other plans for him."

"I miss him."

"I know." She held him close as he began to sob as he hadn't when his *daed* died. Too late she'd realized she should have known the boy needed to mourn his *daed* instead of trying to step into his shoes.

Shoes that were too large for a twelve-year-old who vacillated between being a toddler and a teen and wasn't either.

She held Theo until he cried himself to sleep. Leaning him against the buggy, she stood, shaking her arm that tingled with pins and needles. Her stomach growled, but she ignored it. If she had to go to bed tonight without her supper, she wouldn't complain.

Looking around the barn, she noticed the flashlight's beam was dimming. Once it was gone, they'd be stuck in darkness until the storm was past. Then she realized the flashlight wasn't losing power. The flames consuming the house had already been beat back by the snow and ice.

"How's Theo doing?" Mark asked as he patted the hay bale where he was sitting.

"He's asleep." She perched on its edge and glanced up as the wind scraped across the roof again. Something shifted on it.

"Don't worry," he said. "*This* roof is in *gut* repair. We might lose a few shingles, but it's not going to fall in on us. I think we're hearing debris shifting up there. If the wind keeps up like this, anything that landed on the roof will be blown off by sunrise."

"I've been praying the barn will stay in one piece."

"And praying for help with Theo."

She nodded and leaned against the bales of hay behind them. "I never imagined he wasn't being honest about spending time with Daryn."

"I never imagined that Daryn was being honest when he told me he hadn't seen Theo. What a pair we are!"

"Now you see why you shouldn't have asked me how to help you with Daryn. I didn't know what was going on right under my nose."

"You helped me with Daryn. I discovered I was talking *at* him as if he were an employee. I should have talked *to* him. If I had hope of us becoming friends as well as brothers, I had to respect him as a person." He leaned forward so his forehead was against hers. "I do remember someone telling me that."

"So why couldn't I remember to do the same with Theo?" She turned to look at her cousin, but Mark's gentle fingers tilted her face toward him.

"You've been doing the best you can. Wasn't it you who told me to learn from my mistakes and try not to make them again?"

"That's what my *daed* used to tell me."

"I don't think I've heard you mention your parents before."

"Of course I have."

"Are you sure?"

"I am." But she wasn't. As she looked out at the un-relenting storm, she wondered why she hadn't realized how she had put aside the *gut* aspects of her past along with the painful parts. "Are you okay?"

"Would you be surprised if I said, '*ja*'?"

"No, but I can tell you aren't okay."

He sighed. "I can't fool you, Kirsten. I've convinced Daryn everything's going to be fine, but I don't know what's going to happen. We don't have a place to live, and I don't know how I can afford the materials to re-build."

"You know the community will help."

"It's a lot to ask."

"Not when you would do everything you could to help if someone else's house had been destroyed." She saw him wince and began to apologize for being too plainspoken.

"No, don't say you're sorry. It's not going to help if I hide my head in a hole in the ground like an ostrich."

"Well, you do have a hole in the ground." She put her hands over her mouth, unable to believe she'd let those words escape her lips.

He looked at her, and his lips twitched. Then he laughed and flung his arm around her shoulder.

Kirsten began to laugh, too, though she should be apologizing for her thoughtless words. When the kids came over to see what was going on, she invited the boys to sit with them.

"All of us?" asked Roddy, his eyes darting from one face to the next.

"All of us." Mark motioned for them to close the space between them. "It's going to be cold by dawn."

"Is there anything under those tarps at the back of the barn?" Theo asked.

"Mostly old farm equipment. I planned on selling it over the summer, but I never got around to it."

Owen suggested, "We could go out and gather wood and start a fire."

"You want to start a fire in a barn filled with dry hay?" Mark's chuckle was wry. "It would get hot fast. Too hot."

"Told you," Roddy muttered, glowering at his friend.

The other *Englischer* retorted. "I'm not going to say another word."

While the other boys debated what they should do, Kirsten lowered her voice and leaned toward Mark. "The Sea Gull Holiday Cottages are empty, and I've got the keys. If Lulu is okay with it, and I'm sure she'll be, I'll open one of the cottages for you. It'll be close quarters in a single room with one bed and a foldout sofa, but there are a stove and sink and a small fridge in each one. It should work temporarily for you and Daryn."

"Sounds better than sleeping in the cold barn."

"Sounds great!" interjected Daryn. He reached into his pocket and pulled out a cell phone. "Let's call her!" He frowned. "No signal. Must be the storm."

Mark's brows lowered as his eyes focused on the phone. "Where did you—?"

She jabbed an elbow into his ribs where his brother wouldn't see. He should focus on Daryn trying to help instead of asking about the phone.

Mark cleared his throat and asked, as he rubbed the spot where she'd given him that sharp nudge, "Were you listening?"

"It's not as if you were whispering all that quietly."

Daryn's eyes twinkled in the sparse light from the dying flashlight. "When I heard Kirsten mention my name, I assumed you weren't trying to kiss her."

"So you're an expert on wooing ladies?" Mark asked with a hint of humor.

His brother gave him a thumbs-up.

Kirsten smiled as she pulled her coat more tightly around her. The air in the barn, while warmer than outside, was growing colder with each passing minute. The storm howled, and she wondered how long before it blew itself out.

"I'm hungry," Theo said.

"Me, too." Owen clamped his mouth closed and scowled, furious with himself for speaking when he'd vowed not to.

"I wished I'd left the cookies in the buggy," she said. Her stomach grumbled again, and she pressed her hands to it.

"Don't mention cookies." Theo groaned before adding, "My cousin makes the best cookies."

Daryn got up and said, "We don't have to be hungry."

"What do you mean?" asked Mark, aiming the flashlight to follow his brother as he went to a wooden box near the horses' stalls.

Opening the box, Daryn lifted out a backpack. He brought it to them. Sitting, he unzipped it and tipped it up. Food fell out.

"What's this?" Mark asked as he picked up a jar of peanut butter.

"My stash. In case you kicked me out, and I had to find my way home."

"I wouldn't have kicked you out."

"I wasn't sure about that." He wedged the heel of his boot between two boards and stared at it. "Especially at first when you didn't think about me other than how much work I could do for you."

"You're right."

Kirsten saw Daryn was as astonished as she was by Mark's words. Neither of them spoke as Mark went on.

"I thought hard work would keep you from getting into trouble. *Daed* never worked us hard, and that left plenty of time to find other things to do. That gave time for our brothers and sisters to find mischief."

"Everyone but you. You never got in trouble."

"Maybe I should have."

"What?" Daryn's voice rose two octaves in a squeak. "You think you *should* have gotten into trouble?"

"My life was focused on work. Nothing else. All work and no play… Well, you know the rest."

Kirsten put her hand on his sleeve, then let it slide down so her fingers could entwine with his. She guessed Daryn had no idea how huge an admission this was for Mark because the teen opened the peanut butter and pulled out a loaf of bread. Handing both to Theo, he was reaching for a box of fruity candy when something hammered on the door.

The kids froze, but Kirsten rose along with Mark. He motioned for the boys to stay where they were as he carried the flashlight toward the window. Peering out, he gasped as light flashed through the glass.

Another propane tank exploding?

No, the flashes were red and blue and yellow.

Kirsten ran to the door and lifted the latch. Hands on the edge rolled the door open. Snowflakes, sharpened by the storm, pelted her, and she recoiled.

She was seized and pushed into the barn. In disbe-lief, she stared at a dozen people dressed in first responder uniforms. Royal Canadian Mounted Police and firefighters.

A woman stepped forward, dressed like the other firefighters. Her badge identified her as the fire chief. "Was anyone in the house when it blew up?"

"It collapsed first," Theo said, bouncing over to stand by Kirsten.

"No one was in the house." Mark drew Kirsten and Theo out of the wind. "We escaped before it collapsed and the propane tank blew."

The woman turned to the other firefighters. "Let them know it's okay to let it burn as long as it doesn't spread."

Kirsten was pretty sure the Mountie was Constable Boulanger. He looked past her to the two *Englisch* boys and frowned. "What's your part in this?"

"Can't that wait?" Mark asked. "These kids are cold."

The constable nodded. "We'll get everyone to—"

Kirsten interrupted, "My *aenti*'s house is close. Helga Petersheim."

"She called in the alarm," the fire chief said. "We arranged to follow a snowplow out here. Are you her niece?"

"Ja." She put her arm around Theo. "This is her son."

"I'm the fire chief, Kelsey Davenport, if you need me," she said. "I don't think you will because I'm leaving you in Constable Boulanger's competent hands. I want to make sure the wind doesn't give that fire a second life."

The constable didn't wait for the fire chief to leave before he told them to gather their things and prepare to head out into the storm. He herded them outside, not giving Kirsten a chance to talk to Mark again. Another officer appeared out of the storm, and the *Englisch* boys and the Yutzys were led to one vehicle while she and Theo were taken to the constable's.

The warmth inside it was welcoming, but as he drove them along the road that looked as if it hadn't been plowed as the snow fell even faster, the car's heater couldn't touch the iciness within her. She hadn't been completely honest with Mark. Not truly. If he learned of her past, he'd pity her like everyone else did. That was one thing she couldn't endure—having the man she loved pitying her.

Chapter Fifteen

Mark looked out the door of the cottage on Christmas Eve and wasn't surprised to see it was snowing. Not like the blizzard last week, but a soft, wafting snow where each flake seemed to dance in midair. Cold seeped off the bay, but after days of frigid weather, the air seemed balmy as the temperatures hovered around zero.

For the past nine nights, he and Daryn had slept at Sea Gull Holiday Cottages. Their cottage was the farthest from the bay. With the ground covered with snow and the water frozen, a view and the accompanying wind was the last thing he'd wanted. The tiny cottage was cramped, though they hadn't been able to salvage anything from the burned house.

Every morning, he thanked God for keeping them safe. He tried not to think of what would have happened if the roof had given way while he and Daryn slept. Mark still woke out of a deep sleep almost every night with nightmares of someone calling to him from the rubble.

Kirsten. Hers was the voice he heard most often. If he'd lost her...

That had been the second time he'd risked losing her.

The first time had been his fault. He never should have listened to Lucas and Juan when they urged him to practice flirting with other women to make Kirsten jealous. He'd endeavored to be honest with others throughout his life, and he shouldn't have listened to the advice Juan and Lucas had told him was foolproof. Well, it was clear he was the fool, and he'd found proof of it!

Mark walked to the table that was only two steps away and picked up his cup. The *kaffi* inside was growing cold, like everything else in the cottage. He doubted there was much insulation in the walls because it was intended for guests to enjoy during the Island's short summer. He had to count himself blessed to have a place to stay with a roof that remained over his head. The farm was a short walk away, and after the new year began, rebuilding his house would get underway as well.

Ordering enough lumber and other supplies meant a wait on the Island, but at least the Confederation Bridge had reopened in the wake of the storm. Twenty-five years ago, he would have had to stay at the cottage until spring because the ferry crossing to the island only ran after the ice broke.

The community would raise the house and put a roof on it. He'd finish the interior, working when he could around planting next year's crop. He glanced toward the bathroom door where he could hear his youngest brother getting ready for church. Because Christmas was on a Sunday this year, their church service was being held the day before. Christmas among the plain folks was a day for family.

Daryn gulped down the last of the cookies donated from the cookie exchange last Saturday; then they left for the services which were at Lucas's farm. Yesterday, Mark and Daryn had helped their cousins prepare the house for the *Leit* to come together for worship. In Mark's opinion, the house that Juan and Lucas shared while they were working to make the house on Juan's farm habitable had looked like an explosion had happened in it, too. Clothing, clean and worn mixed together, had been scattered over every flat service except where dirty dishes were piled. The clothes had been taken upstairs to be left on an extra bed, and Juan had tackled the dishes with Daryn's help while Mark worked with Lucas to get rid of dust and dirt and leaves that had been tracked in before the snow arrived.

More than once, Daryn had suggested his cousins hire Ocean Breezes Cleaning Service to take care of their house. Nobody had seemed surprised when Mark offered to speak to Kirsten to find out if she had time for another client.

It was an excuse to talk to her after the service, but an odd sorrow draped over him when he realized he had to have an excuse. Before the benefit supper, he would have simply sought her out. He would have enjoyed her company, and they would have challenged each other and laughed together and his thoughts would have been filled with images of him drawing her close as her eyes closed and his lips found hers. Thoughts that had been thwarted at every turn.

"Ready to brave the elements?" Daryn asked with a smile. His brother hadn't hidden his eagerness to spend the day with Janelle.

Mark had learned not to ask probing questions, giving his brother room to make his own decisions and his own mistakes. He was striving to change, and Daryn could see he was trying. That seemed to be enough for them to find more common ground every day.

The walk took longer than Mark had guessed with the snow knee-deep in places. The first hymn was already underway when they slipped into the house and found two seats on the men's side. He looked over the head of the shorter man in front of him and caught Kirsten's eyes. When a faint smile warmed her face, he lowered his gaze before he couldn't keep from jumping over the low benches and sweeping her into his arms right in the middle of the service.

Danki, *God, for keeping her safe,* he prayed as he had so many times since his house was destroyed.

The prayer kept repeating through Mark's mind during the three-hour-long service. As soon as he could after the meal was served, he slipped away, heading across the field to his farm. It didn't take long for him to hitch up the horses and drive to Lucas's place.

Exclamations rang out as he slowed the antique red-and-green sleigh with its remnants of gold trim in front of his cousin's house, bringing it to a stop near where Kirsten was coming out onto the porch.

"Where did you find that?" she asked, her gaze sweeping over the ornate sleigh.

"In the barn." He grinned as he stepped out. "It was under the tarps."

"You said that was old farm equipment."

"I said it was *mostly* old farm equipment." He swept his arm toward the sleigh. "Would you like to try it out? I thought I'd save you a cold walk home."

"By offering me a cold ride home?"

He didn't have a chance to answer her teasing because Theo popped out of the house and asked, "Can we go, too?"

He was about to say no, then saw Kirsten's happiness. She was thrilled to see the boy acting with the unbridled enthusiasm of his age instead of trying to keep up with older, *Englisch* boys. It took every bit of Mark's willpower to make his lips form the single word, "Sure."

Theo scrambled onto the back seat of the sleigh along with his sister and Daryn. A single glance from Kirsten was enough to keep Janelle from trying to ease past her brother to sit next to Daryn. Theo earned a glower from his sister, but didn't shift from his spot in the middle. Janelle must have given up because the youngsters' conversation began again, each one trying to talk over the other.

Mark realized Kirsten hadn't accepted his invitation. "Do you want to join us?"

She nodded, and her eyes sparkled like the sunshine on the snow in the open fields.

Helping her in, Mark retook his place. He draped a blanket over their knees, then drew it back a few inches. "See? There are warm coals in the heater."

She laughed. "You've arranged for everything."

Except for three kids in the back seat, he thought as he picked up the reins. The rest of the *Leit* cheered as the horses pulled the sleigh out onto the snowy road between his cousins' farms. The kids waved to their friends and neighbors.

"Is Theo doing better?" Mark asked beneath the chatter from the rear. "It's *gut* to see him smiling."

"He's doing okay. He feels better after talking to the police. He was chastened by the court-appointed social worker who's working with him to find community service he can do."

"I thought they were going to have to repaint the boats they vandalized."

She smiled. "They are, but his social worker wants him to do other work as well."

"Something he'll find so annoying he won't let himself be led into trouble again."

"It's more that she wants to give him time to speak with a therapist about how he's doing since *Onkel* Stanley died. She believes it will help him. At least, that's the hope."

He squeezed her hand under the blanket and smiled. "It's a *gut* hope."

Mark kept smiling as the sleigh cut through the snow. When they reached the main road, he turned onto the verge between the snow piles where the plows had cleared the tarmac.

This was not going how he'd hoped it would when he came up with his plan last night. He hadn't imagined three kids would be chattering in the rear seat. Slowing the sleigh, he said, "It looks as if the ice on the bay is strong enough for skating."

As he'd hoped, Theo began clamoring to get his skates and play hockey. Mark kept his grin to himself when Daryn and Janelle chimed in, wanting to get out on the ice. He didn't wait for Kirsten to give her permission before he said, "That sounds like a *wunderbaar* idea. Daryn, make sure none of you go where the ice is thin."

"Ja!" His brother jumped out of the sleigh along with the Petersheim kids. They split in two directions to get their equipment, shouting that they'd meet on the shore in five minutes.

As the *kinder* ran along the road, Kirsten asked, "Daryn's skates survived?"

"They were in the barn along with his hockey stick." Mark chuckled. "He doesn't seem to mind we lost everything in the house as long as he has his sports equipment."

"It's nice to know where his priorities are."

"That's one thing about us Yutzy men. We know what's truly important." He raised his hand and brushed her soft cheek with his fingertips. When she gasped, he started to draw back. Then he saw the delight in her eyes. It emboldened him to say what he'd hoped he'd have the chance to say, "If you're willing, I'd like my Christmas present now."

Kirsten stared at Mark as she echoed, "Christmas present?" Why was he expecting a gift from her for Christmas? The plain people, once they were adults, seldom exchanged gifts at Christmas. She'd bought each of her cousins a small token, new gloves for Janelle and a book by his favorite author for Theo, the latter because *Aenti* Helga had insisted he go nowhere but to school, his community service obligations and home every day for the next month.

Christmas was for being together with family and celebrating Jesus's birth. A meal that left everyone filled to the brim was the highlight of the day, not opening gifts.

"Ja," he said, as he leaned toward her. "Will you give me the gift I want most for Christmas this year? Will you marry me, Kirsten?"

Marry him? Her heart danced with joy before crashing. She'd said, *"Ja"* when asked this before…and it had led to disaster. Not that she thought Mark was as fickle as Eldon Wheeler, but she couldn't trust herself.

"You're not answering." His smile was turning into a taut caricature of itself. "If you don't want to marry me, just say so."

"It's not…" Her voice broke on the two words, so she cleared her throat and began anew. "It's not that I don't want to marry you—"

"Because there's someone else."

"Four someone elses."

"What?" His voice rose on the single word. "You're walking out with four other men?"

"Not now." She put her hand on his sleeve to forestall his next question. "I haven't been honest with you about my past, Mark."

"You haven't said much about it."

"I know." She lowered her eyes, unable to meet his when they were filled with hurt. "I don't like to talk about what happened. I didn't want to lie, but speaking the truth is painful."

"I don't want to cause you pain, Kirsten. *Ich liebe dich.*"

Joy rushed through her as he spoke of loving her. The words that she loved him, too, burned on her lips, but she remained silent.

He took her gloved hands and held them between his. "Will you tell me?"

Thinking of how she'd told Theo he had to be honest, she knew she must be the same. Taking a steadying breath, she related how her heart had been broken four times. She watched his face as he listened without comment.

"That's why you came to Prince Edward Island?" he asked.

"Ja." Frustration blossomed within her because she couldn't guess what he was thinking because his voice was as bland as his expression.

"Because you didn't want to see those men again?"

"Because I didn't want everyone looking at me with sad expressions." She flipped her hand in a careless gesture. "Oh, there goes poor Kirsten Petersheim. She stood up to get married, and there wasn't a groom for her. What did she do to cause Eldon Wheeler to run away from her?"

"So you decided to run away, too?"

"No… I mean, *ja*. It was clear to me God didn't want me to make a life there."

"And you hopped the first train out of Dodge?"

"What?"

He waved aside her question. "It's an *Englisch* saying. It means you ran away as quickly as you could."

"I did. *Aenti* Helga and *Onkel* Stanley were coming to Prince Edward Island, so I decided to join them. I hoped the talk wouldn't follow me here."

"I realize now why I hurt you at the benefit." He gave her a weak smile. "Also why you turned down my invitation. I've been racking my brain trying to figure it out."

"I should have told you."

He nodded. "I understand why you didn't. You know how important it is to me not to fail at anything I attempt."

"I might have noticed that."

He chuckled at her droll tone. "I thought you might have, but what I never noticed was how important it was to you not to fail either."

"Me?"

"You've been doing your best to hide what you see as your failures. I have a lot to learn, but I know we don't have to try to measure up to anyone's expectations except God's." He stroked her fingers as he said, "I want to share a prayer that has helped me. 'Show me how to hand control over to You, God. Show me the way to relinquish my need to manage everything…and live the life You've chosen for me.'" He gazed into her eyes, and she found she was looking into the depths of his heart as he laid it bare for her. "For years, I've thought *I* was in control of my life. What a fool I was! I've never been in control. God has been."

"I try to remind myself, too, when it's quiet and my thoughts plague me."

When he laughed, she asked, "You think my humiliation is funny?"

"I'm not laughing at your feelings, Kirsten. I'd never do that." He pressed a quick kiss on her lips, leaving her breathless. "I'm laughing at those four fools. Each of them passed up his chance to spend the rest of his life with the most *wunderbaar* woman in the world. I'm glad the Lord closed their eyes to the truth so it's possible you could be mine. Won't you say *ja* and marry me?"

Again she paused, but she didn't look away. She wanted him to see the love shining from her heart.

Love.

This was love, the real thing. Not what she'd believed she was feeling four times before. That emotion had been tepid and flavorless compared to the feast of sensations she experienced each time her heart reached out to his.

"Ja," she whispered.

Epilogue

The following May...

"A letter for you, Mrs. Yutzy."

Kirsten smiled as she looked up from where she was kneading the bread that she'd put into the oven to rise one more time before she baked it for tomorrow's breakfast. The new kitchen in the new house smelled of fresh paint. The rooms upstairs waited to be finished, but there had been enough completed for her to move in as Mark's wife more than a month ago. "I like the sound of that."

"The letter?"

She sent a pinch of flour in his direction. He batted at it as if it were swirling snow.

"You know what I mean," she said with a laugh, glad that the winter was past and they had the whole summer to look forward to together. She was beginning to suspect maybe in the winter, they'd have a reason to celebrate. She wasn't certain yet, but she intended to speak to her *aenti* and get her opinion. She couldn't wait to share with Mark that he'd be a *daed* early next year.

Realizing he was waiting for her to continue, she said, "I mean I like the part about being Mrs. Yutzy."

"I like it too." As she turned to put the bread in the unlit oven to rise, he added, "You said this is your *mamm*'s recipe, ain't so? So why are you making it to take to her?"

"Because she likes how I bake it." Kirsten checked the marbled bread was centered in the oven before she closed the door. "*Daed* doesn't like this kind of bread."

"Which is why you made him dozens of cookies." He chuckled. "You need to leave room in the van for what the rest of us are bringing."

"There are only five of us going to Ontario." She smiled as she thought of how excited her cousins and *Aenti* Helga were to see old friends and family. "There will be plenty of room for Daryn on the way back."

His smile broadened as it did every time anyone mentioned Daryn. After returning home and taking a job in the woodworking shop, Daryn had decided to rejoin Mark in Prince Edward Island. The boy still planned to head west some day and work on a ranch, but he'd decided to learn more about farming first.

Kirsten thought, but didn't say, it was an elaborate excuse when it was obvious to her Daryn and Janelle missed each other. They were too young to marry, but not too young to spend time together, taking the time she never did before coming to Prince Edward Island to decide if someone was the right match for the rest of their lives. She admired her cousin for not jumping in as Kirsten had, so desperate to prove to her parents that she could meet their expectations.

She picked up the letter and gasped.

"What is it?" asked Mark.

"It's from a friend in Ontario." She blinked sudden

tears. She'd given up ever hearing from Gwendolyn when her friend hadn't written back after marrying Nolan Oatney. "Gwendolyn Oatney." Not a twinge taunted her when she spoke her friend's married name.

"Aren't you going to open it?"

"Ja," she said, but continued to stare at the envelope.

"If you want to be alone to open it, I can leave."

"No, no." She put her fingers on his sleeve and wondered if she'd ever get accustomed to that zing of happiness each time she touched him. She hoped not. With a gasp, she drew back her hand. "Oh, I got flour on your shirt."

"It brushes off." He glanced at the letter and curved his hand along her face. "I'm here if you need me."

"I know that." She kissed his cheek. "And I love that."

The note was short. Gwendolyn had heard that Kirsten and her new husband were coming for a visit, and she hoped there would be time for her and Kirsten to get together. Sharing that with Mark, she turned the page over and read the rest.

"What is it?" Mark asked. Her amazement must have been visible on her face.

"Gwendolyn wrote that Eldon Wheeler is back."

"The man who asked you to marry him and then vanished?"

She nodded. "She says his leaving didn't have anything to do with me. He jumped the fence." She sighed. "That must have difficult for his parents."

"Because he was put under the *bann*?"

"Ja. For a year, they didn't know where he was. He's come home and made things right with his family and his bishop. He's been asking where I am."

"So he can apologize to you?" His face was taut, drawing his mouth into a straight line.

"Why else?"

"He could be hoping to convince you to give him another chance."

"I'm sure you're wrong about that."

His smile returned. "Whether he's hoping for a reconciliation or not, *I'm* sure of one thing."

"What's that?"

"He's too late." He wrapped his arms around her and drew her lips to his. Her laugh became a happy sigh as she melted into his embrace, the place where she was meant to be.

Forever...

* * * * *

If you enjoyed this story,
don't miss these other books from Jo Ann Brown:

Find more great reads at www.LoveInspired.com

Dear Reader,

Welcome back to Prince Edward Island...just in time for Christmas! As the seasons change, so can the most stubborn hearts, including the hearts belonging to Kirsten Petersheim and Mark Yutzy. Do you ever find yourself worrying too much about what other people think of you? I do, even though I know the only ones who should matter are my loved ones and God. Kirsten and Mark both share this worry, judging themselves by how others perceive them. Until they can accept themselves for the special and unique people they are, they'll never have that happy-ever-after ending they're both yearning to share.

Visit me at www.joannbrownbooks.com And look for my next book set on Prince Edward Island coming soon!

Wishing you many blessings,
Jo Ann Brown

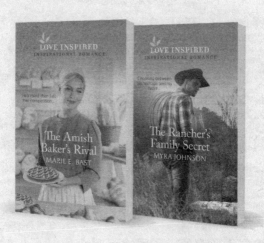

COMING NEXT MONTH FROM
Love Inspired

CHRISTMAS ON HIS DOORSTEP
North Country Amish • by Patricia Davids

To save her sister's puppy from their legal guardian's wrath, Jane Christner drops the dog off on the doorstep of neighbor Danny Coblentz. The Amish teacher is determined to help Jane and her sister find a better life in his community this Christmas. Could it also lead to love?

AN AMISH CHRISTMAS WISH
Secret Amish Babies • by Leigh Bale

Newly widowed, Seth Lehman needs help caring for his nine-month-old daughter. He offers Susanna Glick free use of his empty storefront for her noodle business if she'll also watch baby Miriam while he tends both their farms. But as Christmas draws closer, their arrangement begins to feel like a family...

AN ALASKAN CHRISTMAS PROMISE
K-9 Companions • by Belle Calhoune

Kit O'Malley is losing her sight and begs local rancher Leo Duggan to let her have one of the service puppies he's training. As they work together, the single mom gains hope of a more normal life, but there's a secret that could tear them apart...

A CHRISTMAS BARGAIN
Hope Crossing • by Mindy Obenhaus

When single mom Annalise Grant inherits a Texas Christmas tree farm and discovers a portion of her trees are on her neighbor's property, she'll do anything to hold on to them—including suggesting a collaboration with the handsome rancher next door. Will a compromise turn into the family neither expected?

HER CHRISTMAS REDEMPTION
by Toni Shiloh

After a past riddled with mistakes, Vivian Dupre needs a second chance in her new town—and helping with the church's Christmas Wishes program is the best place to start. But as she and Michael Wood work to fulfill wishes, can Vivian keep her secrets from thwarting her own holiday dreams?

A SECRET CHRISTMAS FAMILY
Second Chance Blessings • by Jenna Mindel

Ruth Miller and Bo Harris enter a modern-day—and secret—marriage of convenience to save Ruth's home as well as her late husband's business. Despite their intention to keep the relationship strictly business, love starts to bloom. But the truth about Ruth's first husband might shatter their fragile marriage deal forever.

LOOK FOR THESE AND OTHER LOVE INSPIRED BOOKS WHEREVER BOOKS ARE SOLD, INCLUDING MOST BOOKSTORES, SUPERMARKETS, DISCOUNT STORES AND DRUGSTORES.

LICNM1022

Get 4 FREE REWARDS!

We'll send you 2 FREE Books plus 2 FREE Mystery Gifts.

FREE Value Over **$20**

Both the **Love Inspired®** and **Love Inspired®** **Suspense** series feature compelling novels filled with inspirational romance, faith, forgiveness, and hope.

HARLEQUIN
PLUS

Announcing a **BRAND-NEW** multimedia subscription service for romance fans like you!

Read, Watch and Play.

Experience the easiest way to get the romance content you crave.

Start your **FREE 7 DAY TRIAL** at
<u>www.harlequinplus.com/freetrial</u>.

SPECIAL EXCERPT FROM

LOVE INSPIRED
INSPIRATIONAL ROMANCE

When a service dog brings them together,
will secrets tear them apart?

Read on for a sneak preview of
An Alaskan Christmas Promise
by Belle Calhoune.

Kit O'Malley gripped the steering wheel tightly as she navigated down the snow-covered Alaskan roads. Her recent medical diagnosis had turned her life upside down, and now all she could think about was losing her eyesight. Kit didn't believe anything could ever fully prepare a person for such a blow.

She'd confided her diagnosis to her sister, who'd told her about Leo Duggan's work with service dogs. Jules had encouraged her to seek out Leo to see if she could adopt one of his canines. Ever since, Kit had been holding on to the idea like a lifeline.

She had never considered herself to be particularly brave, but over the past few weeks she'd been feeling extremely vulnerable and weak. At the moment she needed to focus on the matter at hand—beseeching Leo to consider her request.

As she approached the Duggan Ranch, Kit drove up to a gate emblazoned with a big *D* on it. Up ahead Kit spotted horses standing outside in an enclosure. She wasn't certain, but she thought this might be where Leo was working with the service animals.

Once she stepped inside the stables, an adorable yellow Labrador puppy bounded toward her, enthusiastically wagging its tail as it reached her side.

"Well, hello there," Kit said. She wished she could pet the dog, but she'd once heard that service dogs shouldn't be touched or interacted with.

"Jupiter, come back here." A deep commanding voice called out to the dog, causing it to run straight back to Leo. With a single hand motion, he had the pup sitting at his feet and gazing up at him with adoration.

"I'm so sorry if I interrupted your session," Kit apologized.

"Hey there, Kit," he said, his voice full of surprise. "No worries. I'm not training at the moment." He knit his brows together. "What brings you out to the ranch?"

She swallowed past her nervousness. "I heard about the dogs you're training as service animals, and I wanted to know if I could adopt one."

Don't miss
An Alaskan Christmas Promise *by Belle Calhoune,*
available December 2022
wherever Love Inspired books and ebooks are sold.

LoveInspired.com